Smoke on the Wind

A Kaya Classic
Volume 2

by Janet Shaw

✦ American Girl®

For my daughter, Kris,
her husband, Paul, and
their sons, Will and Peter,
with love

To my stepdaughter, Betsy,
and Ted, with love

To my stepdaughter, Becky,
and her children,
Tony and Adrienne,
with love

Beforever

Beforever is about making connections.
It's about exploring the past, finding your
place in the present, and thinking about the
possibilities your future can bring. And it's about
seeing the common thread that ties girls from
all times together. The inspiring characters you
will meet stand up for what they care about
most: Helping others. Protecting the earth.
Overcoming injustice. Through their courageous
stories, discover how staying true to your own
beliefs will help make your world better
today—and tomorrow.

❋TABLE *of* CONTENTS ❋

Kaya and her family are *Nimíipuu*, known today as Nez Perce Indians. They speak the Nez Perce language, so you'll see some Nez Perce words in this book. "Kaya" is short for the Nez Perce name *Kaya'aton'my'*, which means "she who arranges rocks." You'll find the meanings and pronunciations of these and other Nez Perce words in the glossary on page 174.

A Starving Dog

s Kaya helped her mother and grandmother set up the tepee poles and cover them with tule mats, she heard the *honk! honk! honk!* of geese flying high overhead. She stopped work, shaded her eyes, and gazed up into the deep blue sky. Flocks of geese, swans, herons, and cranes were flying northward from their wintering grounds in the south. As she listened to the noisy chorus of their cries, she heard other sounds, too. The warm spring wind gusted across the rolling hills, rustling the greening prairie grasses. Larks and swallows called softly while they built their nests. Her bothersome little brothers laughed and squealed as they scampered about with the other children. She heard her grandfather sigh with pleasure when he tilted up his face to the warm sun that eased the aches in his bones. Everything

Kaya heard joined in the song of new life returning to
the land.

After the long, cold winter, Kaya and her family
had left the sheltered canyons of Salmon River Country
and journeyed upland to dig fresh kouse roots, the
delicious, nourishing food her people needed. This
spring they'd come to the beautiful Palouse Prairie,
where they'd met *Nimíipuu* and other peoples with
whom they shared these root fields. There would be
many reunions with friends, and much trading,
dancing, games, and horse racing, too. But Kaya's
family had chosen to come here for another reason—
they'd promised to help Two Hawks, the boy who had
escaped with Kaya from enemies while in Buffalo
Country. He needed to get back to his own people, the
Salish. Salish often came to the Palouse Prairie to dig
roots and trade. A trader might take Two Hawks to his
home. Kaya looked around for Two Hawks. He was
herding horses with some other boys. She thought he
looked happy, but she knew he badly missed his family.

Her grandmother touched Kaya's arm. Kaya started.
She'd let her attention wander.

"Why are you watching the boys when you should

be working?" *Kautsa* asked. Her usually gentle voice
was stern. "And you're frowning. What have I taught
you about making yourself ready to dig roots?"

"You've told me not to have bad thoughts that
might make the roots hide themselves," Kaya said.
"And I must stay away from sad thoughts, too, so the
roots won't make us sick when we eat them."

"*Aa-heh*," Kautsa said. "You must have a pure
heart to do your work well and be worthy of your
namesake."

Kaya knew her grandmother was right, but she'd
found that staying away from bad or sad thoughts
was very, very difficult. Her younger sister, Speaking
Rain, was still a captive of enemies from Buffalo
Country. Kaya's horse had been captured, too, and
then traded away. And each time Kaya thought of
Swan Circling's death, she had to fight to keep her
heart from aching. Swan Circling had been a respected
warrior woman, and she had wanted Kaya to have her
name, the greatest gift a person could give. Kaya hoped
that one day she'd feel ready to use it. Sometimes, just
for a moment, Kaya wished she could be a carefree
child again, like her twin brothers, who were happily

trying to sneak up on green racers and catch the little snakes with their bare hands.

"Will the root digging begin soon?" Kaya asked.

"Very soon!" Kautsa said with a smile. "Two women elders went to check the fields today. They came back with good news. The roots are waiting for us. The roots are singing!"

Kaya felt a shiver down her back. *Hun-ya-wat*, the Creator, sent both animals and plants so that Nimíipuu might have food to live. But if anyone treated these gifts disrespectfully, then the fish, the deer, the berries, or the roots might not give themselves to The People. Kaya prayed that nothing she had said or done—or thought—would cause her people to go hungry.

Kautsa put her strong arm around Kaya's shoulder. "I see that something troubles you, Granddaughter." Now she spoke gently, as if she understood Kaya's troubled thoughts.

"I still have a lot of sadness in me," Kaya admitted. "Do you think I should keep away from the digging?"

"Only you know your own heart," Kautsa said.

"I want to work with you and the others!" Kaya

blurted. "I want to do my part, like my namesake always did."

"Of course you do!" Kautsa said. She squeezed Kaya to her, then held her at arm's length to look at her. "But you've told me your heart is troubled. For now, let others work with the food until your dark thoughts leave you and the time of mourning is over in your heart. You can join us when your thoughts are clear again."

"Aa-heh," Kaya said with a sigh. She knew her grandmother's advice was wise, but the realization that she wouldn't be working with the other girls and women made her feel even lonelier.

Kautsa glanced at the sun, high overhead. "We need firewood so I can get our meal started," she said.

"I'll get some," Kaya said at once. She was glad to walk across the greening field to the stream, which was rushing with the runoff of melted snow. As she went, she saw horses rolling on their backs to shed their thick winter coats. When she bent to pick up driftwood, she saw the first early blooms of yellowbells. Soon her thoughts were lighter, but still she felt uneasy, as if she were being watched. Were the Stick People peeking at

her? Was a bear prowling nearby, hungry after its long
winter sleep? She stood and looked around.

Kaya's father had taught her that even the smallest
of signs carry big messages. He'd taught her to look for
the tip of a deer's antler, or the tremble of a branch after
an elk has passed. So Kaya let her gaze move slowly
across the scrub brush, searching for any little sign
of what might be hidden there. In a moment, she saw
the amber glint of two eyes watching her through the
leaves. Those eyes reminded her of something—what?
Then she remembered the yellow eyes of the wolf that
had led her through the snowstorm toward her father
when she was stranded on the Buffalo Trail. But a wolf
wouldn't come so close to where people camped. She
crouched. Now she made out a pale muzzle and a black
nose, the head of a large dog.

Drawn by the dog's searching gaze, Kaya inched
closer. The dog moved slowly out of the bushes toward
her, the tip of its tail wagging slightly. She could see
scars on its back and shoulders. She could also see its
ribs showing plainly, though its belly was swollen with
pups soon to be born. It wasn't one of their camp dogs,
which she knew well. Perhaps it had come here with

another band. But why had it strayed off alone?

Gazing up at Kaya with sad eyes, the dog whined low in its throat.

"Are you asking for food?" Kaya said. "I don't have any for you, but your people will feed you. Go back to them. Go!" When she raised her hand, the dog cowered as though afraid Kaya would strike. "Go!" Kaya repeated.

The dog gazed at Kaya for a long moment, perhaps hoping she'd change her mind. Then it slipped away into the bushes, quickly vanishing from sight.

As soon as the dog disappeared, Kaya had the sinking feeling that she'd just done a terrible thing. She remembered that when she and her sister were slaves, fed only on scraps, she'd vowed never again to chase off the starving dogs that sometimes appeared at the camp. This hungry dog had asked for her help, but she'd chased it away. Kaya whistled to call the dog back to her side. But it was too late—the lone dog was gone.

On the day chosen for root digging to begin, the lead diggers rose before first light and went to the sweat lodge to cleanse and purify themselves. Kaya's older sister, Brown Deer, was one of the lead diggers this year. Kaya watched as Brown Deer dressed herself in her best moccasins and her white deerskin dress decorated with elks' teeth and shell beads. Kautsa set Brown Deer's work hat on her head. By the time the lead diggers reached the root fields, the eastern sky bloomed pink as a prairie rose. Soon Kaya heard the women begin to sing the sacred song of thanks for the gift of new food—the root harvest would be a good one! Kaya knew it was right for her to stay away from the digging, but how she longed to wear her own new work hat and to dig with the other women and girls.

As Kaya prepared a morning meal for the twins, she gazed out over the rolling hills, hoping to see the hungry dog she'd chased off. Every day she'd looked for that lone dog, but she hadn't seen it again. How terrible if it had starved to death!

"Little Daughter, I've been looking for you!" *Toe-ta's* deep voice came from behind her. She turned and saw her father gazing kindly at her, as if he understood that she was sad. "I've been thinking that we need to train another horse to pull a travois," he said to her.

"I worked with my namesake when she taught a horse to pull one," Kaya said, always careful not to say the name of the dead aloud.

"*Tawts!*" Toe-ta said. "I can use your help. I think the old gray horse your grandmother used to ride would be a good one to work with. Come with me and we'll put a training harness on it. Bring the twins with you—they can help, too."

Toe-ta tied the gray horse to a bent shrub. While the boys waited impatiently, Kaya and her father looped a rawhide rope around the horse's neck. Long rawhide lines attached to the rope led back to a dried buffalo hide that rested on the ground a few feet behind the horse's hind legs. When the training harness was secure, Toe-ta gestured for Kaya to climb onto the hide to add weight to the drag. The hide was back far enough so that if the horse kicked, its legs wouldn't reach Kaya.

Kaya crawled onto the buffalo hide, sat, and held onto the lines with both hands. Then Toe-ta led the horse forward by the halter, speaking all the while in a low, reassuring voice. But the gray shied and dodged and started to kick at the unaccustomed burden it pulled. Kaya laughed as the buffalo hide bumped and skidded over the smooth ground—this horse wouldn't toss her off! The twins laughed, too—they wanted to ride on that swaying buffalo hide.

After a short time, the horse quieted down and walked steadily as Toe-ta led it around the ring of tepees. At last he drew the horse to a halt and motioned for Kaya to stand up and take the lead rope from him. "You boys get on now," he told the twins, and they eagerly jumped onto the hide as Kaya took hold of the halter.

Toe-ta watched as Kaya led the gentle horse away from the tepees, the little boys grinning as they hung tightly to the rawhide lines. When Toe-ta was satisfied that the work was going well, he nodded. "In a few days, when the horse is accustomed to the feel of the drag, we'll add travois poles to the harness," he said. "Go slowly, Kaya. Walk around the village a few more times, then put the horse back with the herd."

Kaya knew her father had asked her to help train the horse because she couldn't dig roots with the other women and girls. And her father had been wise—her heart was lighter now. Like Swan Circling, Kaya loved to work with the horses. When the training session was over and she took the harness off the gray, she noticed that one of its rear hooves seemed worn and sore. She resolved to make a rawhide shoe to fill with medicine for that sore hoof—another lesson her namesake had taught her.

As Kaya walked back to the village from where the horses grazed, she heard a dog growling nearby. The growl was low and challenging. Kaya went through the brush to see what had alarmed the dog.

On the far side of the hill, she came upon Snow Paws, the big black leader of the village dog pack. His hackles were up, his ears were pricked forward, and his teeth were bared. When he saw Kaya approaching, he snarled more fiercely at something backed up against a rocky outcropping. It wouldn't be a skunk—Snow Paws was much too smart for that. What did he have there?

Kaya parted the bushes. There, beside the rocks, was Lone Dog, the one she'd been searching for. Lone Dog's teeth were bared, and she was growling, too, facing off against the big male. With a glance, Kaya saw that Lone Dog's bones showed even more sharply.

Hunger must have given her courage, for tough old Snow Paws could drive off any dog that approached. Even now he was beginning to bark, and soon he'd charge at Lone Dog and bite her.

This time Kaya wouldn't lose her chance to help the starving dog. She stepped between the two dogs and shook a stick at the barking Snow Paws. "Leave her alone!" she ordered him. "Get away from her! Go on now, get away!"

Growling, Snow Paws backed up a few steps. Maybe he thought Kaya had given him the wrong command. But when she shook the stick again, he reluctantly turned tail and stalked off, looking back over his shoulder.

When Snow Paws had gone, Kaya crouched, holding out her hand for Lone Dog to sniff. But the dog kept near the rocks, where she'd been digging out a den. She gazed warily at Kaya, as if Kaya might take up the attack where the black dog had left it.

"Here, come here," Kaya crooned. "I won't chase you away again." She reached into the bag on her belt and took out the pieces of dried salmon she carried for a quick meal. She held out the fish to Lone Dog.

"Here's a little food for you. Come on, eat it."

Still Lone Dog hesitated, although the scent of fish made her tremble. Her yellow eyes gazed intently into Kaya's.

Kaya placed the fish on the ground and stepped back. "Don't be afraid of me. Take the food," she said.

This time Lone Dog didn't need urging. She sprang forward, snapped up the fish, and gulped it down as she bolted away.

Kaya watched Lone Dog round the outcropping and disappear. "I'll bring you more food," she whispered. "You asked me for help and I'll give it. I promise."

Later that day, Kaya sat beside her grandmother as they worked. Kaya held a circle of thick elk hide on her lap. She was lacing a rawhide drawstring through holes she'd punched along the edge of the hide. When she pulled the drawstring tight, she'd have a round moccasin that would fit over the gray horse's hoof and hold a poultice to heal the sore place.

Kautsa was peeling the skins off roots so they could be dried in the sun. She handed Kaya a cleaned root to eat. Fresh roots were welcome after a season of dried food.

"I have something I want to tell you about a dog," Kaya said.

"You always have stories to tell me," Kautsa said with a smile. With her small stone knife, she peeled off the dark root skins. The pile of pale, clean roots on the tule mat in front of her was growing quickly. "Is this story about a dog fight?"

Kaya looked closely at her grandmother, who always seemed to know so much. "How did you know about the fight?"

"I have ears!" Kautsa said with a laugh. "What happened, Granddaughter?"

"A lone dog came to our village for food," Kaya said. "The dog's starving, and she's going to have pups soon. I felt sorry for her. Snow Paws tried to chase her away—that's the barking you heard. But I made him stop."

Kautsa nodded, thinking. "Snow Paws has been the leader of our pack for a long time," she reminded Kaya. "He's a wise dog, and a strong-hearted one. You remember how he got his name, don't you? When he was hardly more than a pup, a hunter took him along to hunt elk. It was winter, and an avalanche crashed down a cliff and buried the man! Snow Paws dug and dug through the snow until he uncovered the hunter. He saved the man's life. A dog like that is one to be trusted. He must have a reason for trying to chase off this lone dog you speak of."

"Snow Paws might think Lone Dog would take his food," Kaya suggested.

"We give our dogs enough to eat," Kautsa said. "If they're hungry, they know how to hunt for more to fill their bellies."

"But Snow Paws chases off every strange dog, doesn't he?" Kaya asked.

"He lets strange dogs join our pack if they accept him as the leader," Kautsa corrected her. "But he chases off dogs that might be dangerous for some reason. Snow Paws senses these things. Perhaps the lone dog is sick, and might make our dogs sick as well."

"Her eyes are bright and her fur's not falling out," Kaya said. "She doesn't look sick—she looks hungry."

"You told me your story to ask what I think about it, didn't you?" Kautsa said. "I think Snow Paws knows more about this lone dog than you do, Granddaughter, that's what I think."

Kaya bit her lip. Her grandmother was wise in all things. But Kaya had given her promise to Lone Dog. As Kaya did so often, she tried to think what Swan Circling would do if she were here. Kaya decided that if Lone Dog wasn't a menace, Swan Circling certainly wouldn't let her starve.

Newborn Puppies

he next morning Kaya went to the stream as the first rays of sun struck through the blanket of mist hanging over the water. Sandpipers were stepping along the shoreline, and a raccoon searched for crawfish in the shallows. Kaya dipped in her water basket, then drank from her cupped hand. It was a quiet morning, though she could hear the voices of the boys taking their morning swim downstream.

As Kaya drank, she saw Lone Dog appear on a rise a little distance away, then look around warily as she trotted to the stream to drink. Kaya set down her water basket and waited until Lone Dog had drunk her fill. *"Tawts may-we!"* Kaya greeted the dog softly. "Look, here's food for you. I didn't forget." She held out the bone she'd brought with her on the chance she would see the dog.

Lone Dog's ears pricked up and she stood with her head lifted, sniffing all the scents traveling over the water and land. Kaya knew Lone Dog smelled the bone, but she didn't come to take it from Kaya's hand as Kaya had hoped. It wouldn't be easy to earn this dog's trust.

Kaya called again, but this time Lone Dog began to back away. "Don't go," Kaya said. "You need this food."

When Lone Dog hesitated, Kaya put down the bone by the stream. She picked up her water basket and started walking, as if she didn't have a thought for the dog. When she glanced over her shoulder, she saw Lone Dog seize the bone and lope off into the brush with it. In a moment the dog had disappeared.

"Did I just see you feeding a coyote?" Raven called to Kaya. Several other boys laughed. They were running back to the village from their swim, water dripping from their bare arms and their hair. They were full of the energy that the fresh, cold water had given them.

"You know that wasn't a coyote," Kaya said crossly. She walked faster. She wasn't in any mood to be teased by these bothersome boys who swarmed around her like a cloud of gnats.

One of the boys was Fox Tail, who had challenged her to race when they were at *Wallowa*. He gave her a sly grin. "You say it's not a coyote, but it acts like one," he insisted. "Coyotes travel alone, but dogs stay with their pack."

"And it should be guarding the camp," Raven added. "Our dogs are supposed to protect us. That's their job. You shouldn't reward a lazy dog with a bone!"

"My people would chase off a dog that didn't do its work," Two Hawks added. He was one of the gang now.

Kaya gave Two Hawks an angry glance—it wasn't fair that he would criticize her after all they'd been through together. "When that dog gets used to us, she'll join our pack," she said. "You'll see."

"We'll see her get fat on our food, then go her own way!" Raven insisted.

"Aa-heh! Now I know why Kaya likes that dog!" Fox Tail cried. "She likes it because it thinks only of itself—just like a magpie! Isn't that right, Magpie?"

He swung around and walked backward, so he could
see Kaya's burning face as he taunted her.

It took all of Kaya's self-control to keep herself from
giving Fox Tail a swat—or letting a tear slide from her
eye. Would she never outgrow that awful nickname
she'd gotten when she failed to take care of the twins?
Would the others never forget that it was her fault
they'd all been switched? Fiercely, she bit the inside
of her lip so that she wouldn't let her anger, or her
disappointment, show.

"No one can tame a coyote—or a wolf!" Fox Tail
said. "Some girls can't tame a dog, either!" With that,
the laughing boys bounded off.

You're all skunks! Kaya thought. Fighting to be
calm—and to have good thoughts—she trudged back
to the camp.

Each day when all the women and girls went to
dig roots, Kaya put the harness on the gray horse and
trained it to pull the buffalo-hide drag. Its sore hoof
was healing well, and soon she was able to add light-
weight poles to the harness. The gentle horse began to

learn to pull those, too. As Kaya worked with the horse, her mind was on Lone Dog. Would she ever come to trust Kaya?

Kaya looked for Lone Dog every time she went to the stream. She waited on the shore as long as she could, but Lone Dog didn't appear. Where was she? Perhaps Lone Dog had already moved on, as the boys had said she would. The thought that Lone Dog might leave made Kaya sad. With her sister in captivity, Kaya often felt alone—like the dog. She realized she wanted the dog to become her friend.

One morning, as Kaya gazed at the empty shoreline, a thought came to her—perhaps Lone Dog was working on the den she'd begun on the hillside. After Kaya took the water basket she had filled to her tepee, she went looking for that place again.

Kaya was almost upon the den before she saw it. Lone Dog had hollowed out a deep circle beneath a rocky overhang. When Kaya crouched, she made out Lone Dog's yellow eyes gazing over the top of the nest, her face barely visible through the long grass.

"Tawts may-we," Kaya said gently. "I thought I might find you here." She slowly went closer, hoping not to scare off the dog. Lone Dog watched her come. She wasn't wary, or nervous.

Kaya got down on her stomach and looked into the nest where Lone Dog lay. There, snuggled up next to one another against their mother's side, were four little newborn puppies. They were nursing, their paws pushing at their mother's belly. With their stubby legs and big bellies, they looked to Kaya more like ground squirrels than dogs.

Panting heavily, Lone Dog gazed up steadily into Kaya's eyes. She seemed calm and sure of herself now that she'd given birth to her pups.

"What a good mother you are!" Kaya whispered to her. She watched the puppies nurse a little longer, then placed the food she'd brought at the edge of the nest. "Here, you must be hungry, too."

Lone Dog sniffed the meaty bone, then shifted herself and got to her feet so she could eat. When she stood, the puppies lost their hold on her and squealed as they tumbled onto their sides. Their eyes weren't open yet, but they found one another by the warmth of their bodies and crept close together to fall fast asleep.

Lying beside the nest, Lone Dog began to gnaw on

the bone. Suddenly, her ears pricked up and she began to growl.

Kaya looked around. She didn't see anything. "It's all right," she said soothingly. "Your pups are safe."

But now Lone Dog was on her feet, her hackles raised along her back and her tail lifted straight up. She growled again, then lunged partway up the hillside, barking ferociously.

Kaya jumped up, too. Was a cougar after the helpless pups?

Instead of a cat, Kaya saw Snow Paws stalking along the top of the hill. Maybe he was only investigating the new scents, but sometimes male dogs went after newborn pups. He must not harm Lone Dog or her little ones! "Get away! Get!" Kaya commanded him. Lone Dog continued to bark violently to keep him at bay.

Snow Paws bared his teeth, as if he were about to charge Lone Dog. Then he changed his mind. He snarled and began backing off. He didn't want a fight with this fiercely protective mother—or with Kaya, who had seized a thick stick and was shaking it at him.

Even after Snow Paws disappeared, Lone Dog

continued to bark. Only when she was satisfied that
the intruder was gone did she return to her nest.
The puppies had slept peacefully through all the
commotion. Gnawing the bone, Lone Dog lay down
beside them again.

"Aa-heh, you know how to take care of your pups,"
Kaya murmured to her. "I'll come visit you again soon."

"These willow branches must be carried down to
the streamside," Kautsa said to Kaya and Brown Deer.
"We need to build a larger sweat lodge." She handed
the girls bundles of willows and took one on her own
back. They walked downhill to the bank of the stream,
where Kaya's mother was hollowing out a shallow pit
in the gravel.

Each day, in winter as well as summer, Kaya and
the other girls and women bathed in a sweat lodge.
The men and boys did the same. Sweat baths relaxed
them and made them clean and healthy in both body
and spirit.

Kautsa set to work bending willow branches
to form a dome over the pit. Brown Deer and Kaya

did the same, placing the branches so that they followed the four directions. The girls often helped to build a lodge like this one—they put up sweat lodges everywhere they stayed.

"Why are you gazing at the hills instead of doing your work, Daughter?" *Eetsa* asked Kaya. "Here, hold these willows so I can tie them together."

"I was thinking about Lone Dog," Kaya admitted to her mother. "I found the den she made in the hill-side."

"It's too bad that dog doesn't come to live with us," Eetsa said. "She could help guard our camp."

"That's what the boys told me," Kaya said. "They teased me about Lone Dog. They said she thinks only of herself—like a magpie. Like *me*, they meant. They won't let me forget that nickname." Swan Circling had promised that the nickname wouldn't matter so much when Kaya got older—but that day seemed a long time coming.

Kautsa stood upright to rub her sore back with both hands. "Don't you remember the story of how dogs, wolves, and coyotes came to be as they are, Granddaughter?"

"I *think* I remember," Kaya said.

"It's an old, old story," Kautsa went on, weaving and tying willows into the framework again. "Four brothers were roaming the hills together. They were looking everywhere for food, because they were very hungry. When they spotted tepees in a valley, and smelled meat cooking, one of the brothers went down for a closer look. People gave him some meat to eat, and he went running back to the other three brothers and told them what had happened. 'If we go live with people, they'll feed us!' he said. 'We won't go hungry anymore.'

"But the other three brothers didn't agree with him. Two of them said, 'If people feed you, they'll expect you to work hard for them in return. We'd rather go off together and hunt for our own food.' The other brother said, 'I don't need people at all, and I don't need companions, either. I'll go hunt by myself.'

"So the first brother became a dog, and chose to eat our food and do our work," Kautsa continued. "The brother who went off to live all by himself became a coyote. And the two brothers who chose to stay together and hunt as a team became wolves.

Remember, Nimíipuu are like wolves. We're strong
as individuals, but we always work together. That's
how it should be."

"It's not natural for a dog to live all alone," Brown
Deer chimed in.

"She's not all alone anymore," Kaya said. "She's had
her pups, four of them, like the story. But they'll grow
up to be dogs, not coyotes or wolves."

"Daughter, don't be too sure of that," Eetsa warned.
She began laying rye grass thickly over the frame to
create a covering.

"What do you mean?" Kaya asked.

"I mean I've had a glimpse of that dog," Eetsa
said. "She looks to me as if she's got some wolf blood
in her. That would be bad, you know. A dog obeys its
master, but no man can be master to a wolf. If there's
wolf blood in that dog, she might challenge her master.
You said you thought Lone Dog had been beaten—
maybe that's why."

"Aa-heh," Brown Deer agreed. "She might have
bitten a child, or snapped at a baby. She could be
dangerous." She laid more armloads of rye grass onto
the framework.

"I think you should keep away from Lone Dog," Kautsa said firmly. "I think you should stay with the dogs we're sure we can trust."

Kaya felt a stab of dismay in her chest. "There's something I must ask you," she said in a low voice.

"Aa-heh, ask me anything," Kautsa replied. "I'll answer you as I think best."

"I hope you'll allow me to go on feeding Lone Dog," Kaya said carefully. "I gave her my promise that I would help her. Shouldn't I keep my word to a dog, as well as to a person?"

Kautsa picked up several fir boughs and laid them on the floor of the new sweat lodge. She didn't speak as she spread out the sweet-smelling boughs, and Kaya knew her grandmother was considering how best to answer. She held her breath.

Finally Kautsa straightened up and put her hands on her hips. "I think I understand you, Granddaughter. You want to be someone who always keeps her word, and that is right. You may go on feeding Lone Dog, as you promised you would. But I want you to be very, very careful for any sign that she might bite. Take my warning seriously, Granddaughter."

"I will," Kaya said quickly. She felt the ache in her chest ease.

"Tawts!" Kautsa's stern face softened and her dark eyes sparkled. "Now I'd like you to start piling up stones to use in our sweat lodge. Your mother named you for the first thing she saw after you were born—a woman arranging the stones for a sweat lodge like this one. That's your job today, Kaya'aton'my'. Do it well."

More Warnings

very day now, more and more people arrived at the digging fields of the Palouse Prairie. This was a very good place for digging kouse. It was also a very good marketplace for traders. Friends from the north traded skins of bear, beaver, and mink from the mountains where they lived. Friends from the west traded their special cedar bark baskets. In return, Kaya's people traded deer and elk skins and the delicious dried salmon that everyone wanted. And every day Kaya kept a lookout for the arrival of Salish traders—she hoped they'd take Two Hawks back to his family. But, as others arrived, there was no sign of anyone from his country. Weren't they going to come to the Palouse this year?

Kaya visited Lone Dog and her pups every day. Often, as she approached the nest, she found Lone

Dog sitting beside it, gazing in her direction. The dog seemed to be waiting for Kaya now. And sometimes it seemed to her that Lone Dog smiled as she ran the back of her hand along the dog's muzzle. "You know I want to be your friend, don't you?" Kaya asked quietly. And Lone Dog wagged her tail as if to say, *Aa-heh, I want to be your friend, too.*

One morning when Kaya was coming back from visiting Lone Dog and her pups, she heard the crier calling out that a new trader had arrived. He had come from far away, where the Big River flows into the sea. Quickly Kaya's grandfather dressed in his best hide shirt and leggings, wrapped his deerskin robe over his shoulders, and went to meet the man. Her grandfather was a shrewd trader. He took with him camas cakes, buffalo hides, and bundles of tules, things that people from the coast would be sure to want.

All day Kaya looked forward to *Pi-lah-ka*'s return. Her grandfather would have many stories to tell, and he might have heard something about Speaking Rain. Slaves were sometimes traded to other tribes—could her sister have been traded to people from the west?

Pi-lah-ka didn't ride back for a long time. When he

did, there were big packs tied onto his pack horses.

Two Hawks was helping Kaya's father coil up hemp rope for trading. Toe-ta and Two Hawks hurried with Kaya and the others to crowd around Pi-lah-ka. Toe-ta motioned for everyone to be seated. Then Pi-lah-ka opened up a pack and showed them what he'd gotten in trade with the man from the coast. First, he handed around a few special beads he'd gotten in exchange for a fine buffalo hide.

Kaya held one of the precious beads in her palm. It gleamed a deep blue, as if she held a piece of the evening sky. Oh, it was beautiful!

Kautsa held up another blue bead to the light. But instead of smiling, she frowned. "These beads are a lovely color," she said slowly. "But I think our bone and shell beads are best for our clothes. I like the old ways."

"For you, old is always better," Pi-lah-ka teased in his deep voice.

"Old ways are safe ways," Kautsa said stubbornly.

Pi-lah-ka took a very small pouch from his bundle and placed it in her lap. "Then here's something that will please you," he said.

Kautsa opened the pouch and lifted out a strand

of glistening dentalium shells. As she held up the valuable shells for everyone to admire, her face lit up like sun shining after a storm. "You did well!" she said to Pi-lah-ka.

Brown Deer's face was alight, too. "Some of those shells would be beautiful on a dress!" she exclaimed.

"Aa-heh, on a dress for a young woman who hopes to marry soon!" Kautsa added with a smile. "These shells are just the decorations we need."

"The trader told of many beautiful new things," Pi-lah-ka insisted. "He told of cloth dyed the brightest red he'd ever seen."

Kautsa's eyes grew wide. "Where did he see bright red cloth?" she demanded.

"The trader said men in huge boats—men with pale, hairy faces—had such cloth," Pi-lah-ka admitted.

Kautsa folded her arms over her chest and drew herself up tall. "Listen to me. I want to tell you something," she said in her most serious voice.

Toe-ta gestured for everyone to pay attention. Kaya and Brown Deer put down the beads. The twins stopped whispering to Two Hawks and turned toward their grandmother to hear what she had to say.

When Kautsa had everyone's attention, she began
to speak. "One night not long ago, I had a vision. In
my vision, I was holding a piece of bright red cloth.
Then, as I held it, the red cloth vanished, and my hand
was red with blood!" She turned to her husband. "My
vision is a warning—harm will come to us from the
men with pale faces."

Kaya shivered. Her grandmother had told them her
visions before. They were given to her so she could help
protect The People.

Pi-lah-ka and Toe-ta nodded solemnly. They always
respected Kautsa's visions.

But out of the corner of her eye, Kaya saw Two
Hawks turn to look at the arrival of more new traders
riding by with their many pack horses. After a moment,
he jumped to his feet.

"Sit, Two Hawks," Toe-ta said sternly to him. "Pay
attention to your elders."

Two Hawks sat again. Kaya could see that he was
trying to be respectful, but he was almost too excited to
hold still.

"Tell us," Pi-lah-ka said. "What's troubling you?"

"I think those traders are Salish," Two Hawks said.

"They're hauling hide tepee covers like my people use, and I think I recognize that big black horse. Maybe those men know what's happened to my family. Can't we follow them?"

Toe-ta stood up right away. "Get your horse," he told Two Hawks. "Kaya, come with me on my horse. Let's see if these men are Salish." He put his hand on Two Hawks's shoulder. "If they are, we'll trade this boy to them for a worn-out moccasin. That would be an even trade, wouldn't it?"

Two Hawks grinned at Toe-ta's joke. Then his glance caught Kaya's, and his smile dimmed. She saw that he was very happy—and also a little sad. Of course, he wanted to get back to his home again. But now he felt at home with her people, too.

The traders were setting up their camp on the eastern edge of the clusters of tepees. Toe-ta signaled a greeting to them as they rode up. But Two Hawks reined in his horse and circled around behind Toe-ta as if he were feeling shy.

A young trader stepped forward, shading his eyes against the setting sun. Toe-ta threw him the words, *This boy is Salish. Do you know him?*

The trader squinted up at Two Hawks and beckoned for him to ride closer. After a moment, the trader shook his head—it had been a long time since Two Hawks was taken captive, and the man didn't recognize the boy.

But Two Hawks recognized him! He slipped off his horse and ran to the young man. Two Hawks threw his arms around the man's waist and pushed his forehead against his broad shoulder. Then they were both laughing and talking at the same time.

When Kaya and her father joined them, Two Hawks turned to them excitedly. "This is my uncle—my mother's brother!" he cried. "He says my parents are alive and well. My sisters are well, too. He'll take me home with him!"

"Tawts!" Toe-ta said. "Two Hawks, ask your uncle to share a meal with us. We have much to talk over with him."

Eetsa prepared a meal of kouse mush, berries, and deer meat. Afterward, the men talked. Because Two Hawks spoke both Nimíipuu and the Salish language of his people, he acted as interpreter. Sometimes they used sign language, too.

Kaya closely followed what they said. Two Hawks told of his time as a slave of enemies from Buffalo Country, and of his and Kaya's escape, and how Toe-ta had found them on the Buffalo Trail. Young Uncle told of everything that had happened to Two Hawks's family while he was gone from them. Toe-ta made plans to join some Salish men to hunt buffalo in their country to the east, and they agreed to meet again the next day to trade with each other.

Then Toe-ta asked about Speaking Rain. Had Young Uncle seen or heard of his little daughter, a blind girl? She'd been a captive, too, but she might have escaped, or been traded. Was there any news of her?

Young Uncle frowned sadly. *I have not heard of the girl you describe,* he said with his hands.

Kaya clasped her hands tightly to keep from crying. But now Two Hawks turned to look her in the eye. "You helped me and brought me to my family," he said to her. "I give my word that I'll try to find your sister and bring her to you."

Kaya blinked back her unshed tears. Two Hawks

was her friend after all. *"Katsee-yow-yow,"* she said to
him gratefully.

Then Two Hawks and Young Uncle spoke together
for a little while. Two Hawks turned to Toe-ta. "My
uncle gives you his pledge, too," he said. "When it's
time for salmon fishing at Celilo Falls, some of my
people will join your people there. Maybe we'll have
news of your daughter then."

Toe-ta nodded. He threw Young Uncle the words,
Thank you for your help.

Kaya glanced at her mother. Eetsa sat with her head
bowed, her lips pressed tightly together. Kaya saw the
sadness in her father's face, too. She understood that
to lose a child was a terrible thing. And to lose a sister
was terrible as well.

Two Hawks leaned toward Kaya. "I asked my uncle
about your horse with the star on her forehead," he
said. "He hasn't seen your horse, but we'll be on the
lookout."

"Katsee-yow-yow," Kaya murmured a second time.
Then she got to her feet and moved away from the
others.

All the bad news she'd heard tore at her heart, and

soon Two Hawks would be leaving, too. Where could she find comfort? She knelt beside her sleeping place and slipped Speaking Rain's buckskin doll out of her pack. As she clutched the doll to her chest, she thought of Lone Dog. She remembered how Lone Dog had licked Kaya's hands when she'd visited her that morning. So Kaya tucked the doll away again, put some scraps of food into her bag, and headed toward the hillside where Lone Dog had her den.

As Kaya came near the den, she called softly, "Here I am, girl, I'm back again." She saw Lone Dog's gold eyes watching her, then the pale tip of her wagging tail. Kaya knelt and parted the grass in front of the nest. The puppies were sleeping in a heap by their mother's side. Lone Dog lifted her head, pricked her ears, and gazed long and hard into Kaya's eyes.

"Are you telling me you know I'm sad?" Kaya asked the dog softly. She placed the food into the nest, and Lone Dog ate without getting to her feet, as if she didn't want to disturb her sleeping pups.

After Lone Dog had eaten, Kaya leaned closer and

stroked the dog's ears and the soft fur under her jaw. She sank her fingers into the thick coat on her back and scratched. "You always let me touch you now," she said to Lone Dog. "Would you let me touch your puppies? You know I won't hurt them. I'm their friend, too."

Moving slowly, Kaya gently stroked the largest pup's warm head with her fingertip. Would Lone Dog growl her away? Panting lightly, Lone Dog looked on calmly.

Then, as Kaya watched, the pup's eyelids parted for the first time. His milky-blue eyes seemed to be looking right at Kaya, but she knew he was too young to see her yet.

That unseeing gaze reminded Kaya of her blind sister's, and she remembered the lullaby she and Speaking Rain loved so well. "*Ha no nee, ha no nee,*" she sang softly to the puppy. "Here's my precious one, my own, dear little precious one."

As Kaya sang, the other puppies began to stir and whimper, crawling against their mother, wanting more milk. Kaya watched the peaceful scene, the ache in her heart easing. She'd been right to come here.

Crack! A stick broke. Then the long grass bent down and rose again.

Kaya sat up quickly. The twins! She could see the tops of their dark heads in the grass. They were sneaking up the hill, playing hunters with their small bows and arrows.

"Boys!" she hissed. "Stay away! This dog might think you'll hurt her puppies and—"

Wing Feather jumped to his feet. "Puppies!" he cried.

Sparrow sprang upright, too. "Can we see them?" he asked.

Before Kaya could stop them, the boys ran up the slope and fell to their knees beside her. "Keep back!" she said. "Lone Dog doesn't know you!" She held out her arm to keep the boys away from the nest, and they settled down on their heels, gazing wide-eyed at the pups.

"She always protects her puppies," Kaya told the boys. "I'm not sure she'll trust you." If they came too close, would the dog threaten them with a growl, or lunge at them, as she had at Snow Paws?

But Lone Dog didn't seem at all worried by the little

boys. Her gaze took them in, then returned to Kaya. Brown Deer had said Lone Dog might have bitten a child or nipped at a baby. *Surely Brown Deer is wrong*, Kaya thought. *Lone Dog knows the twins are no danger to her pups.*

Sparrow was inching closer to the nest. He reached out toward one of the pups, but Kaya caught his hand in hers. "You mustn't touch them," she said firmly.

"Why not?" Wing Feather asked. "Dogs like to be petted."

Kaya thought for a moment. Lone Dog wasn't like the other dogs. Kaya had come to trust Lone Dog, but others thought she might be dangerous, and Kaya couldn't prove that they were wrong. Her grandmother had warned her to be cautious around the dog—and Kaya must take good care of her little brothers, no matter what.

"Listen to me. I want to tell you something," she said to the twins. She hoped her voice sounded like her grandmother's when she commanded attention.

The twins looked up at her right away.

"Lone Dog trusts me," Kaya said. "That's why she lets you two near her puppies. But I'm not sure what she'd do if I weren't with you. To be safe, you mustn't come here by yourselves. Do you hear my warning?" She looked right into their eyes.

After a moment, the little boys nodded.

"Tawts!" she said to them. "Don't forget what I told you. Now come with me. We need to get back to camp."

Danger for the Pups

❈ CHAPTER 4 ❈

Each morning when Kaya awoke, she
thought first of Lone Dog. She dressed
and left the tepee even before her grandmother began to sing her morning prayers. Kaya loved
spending time with the puppies before the work of the
day began.

"Tawts may-we, Lone Dog!" Kaya called softly
as she approached the den in the early mist. "It's me
again!" Every day a surprise awaited her as the puppies
grew and changed.

After the pups had opened their eyes, they learned
to use their stubby legs to creep about. Once they could
walk around their den, they began sniffing it, too—
and sniffing each other. Then their baby teeth began
to show, and chewing on one another's ears and paws
became their pastime. And soon after they began

to chew, their hearing developed. Now, as Kaya approached them, the puppies turned toward her voice. The largest pup, which she called *Tatlo* because he still made her think of a ground squirrel, peeked over the side of the nest.

"Are you glad to see me?" Kaya asked Lone Dog, who lay among her puppies. Lone Dog's tail wagged as Kaya patted her and then stroked Tatlo's soft little ears.

As Kaya stroked the three other pups, Lone Dog jumped out of the nest and took the bone Kaya had brought her. She carried it off a short way and lay down to chew on it. She was leaving her puppies more and more often, though she still stayed nearby to protect them.

Of course, the puppies didn't like their mother leaving them, even for a little while. They yipped and pawed the sides of the nest, trying to call her back to them. Enjoying her bone, Lone Dog ignored their whimpers and cries.

"Hush, hush," Kaya crooned to them. "Your mother needs a rest. She'll come to you soon enough."

With his paws on the edge of the nest, Tatlo watched Lone Dog contentedly munch the bone. The pup impatiently scratched harder and harder, wanting to follow her. Then he got his hind feet going, too, and managed to creep higher. For a moment he teetered on the edge of the nest, then thrust himself over and tumbled out. His high-pitched yelp brought Lone Dog to his side. She licked her startled pup to calm him.

Tatlo's wail excited the other pups to more frantic yipping. Kaya knew that very soon they'd learn how to follow their brother out of the nest. "How will you take care of the pups when they can roam about?" Kaya mused aloud.

Lone Dog's yellow eyes gazed into hers. She seemed to be saying, *I'll teach them to come back to this safe place if there's trouble.*

Kaya scratched Lone Dog behind her ears. "But what if a coyote trails them?" she asked. "What if a bear finds your den?"

Lone Dog nudged Tatlo back into the nest, then jumped in after him. The pups swarmed over their mother as she lay down again to nurse them. She rested on her side, her eyes still on Kaya. She seemed to be saying, *They'll obey me. Wait, you'll see.*

"I'd like to wait," Kaya said. "But I have to join the

others now. I'll come back as soon as I can."

Kaya ran all the way to the stream, where the
women and girls were splashing in the icy water before
taking their morning sweat bath. Beside the sweat
lodge, a fire burned on the pile of stones, heating them
red-hot. Eetsa was pushing some glowing stones
into the lodge to warm it while the others swam. Kaya
undressed and joined them.

When everyone had crowded into the dimly lit
lodge, Eetsa pulled a deerskin over the doorway. Then
she sprinkled cold water onto the heated stones. They
sizzled and popped, sending up a cloud of steam.
The women and girls joined in a song of thanks and
praise to Grandfather Sweat Lodge for helping them
and guarding them against illness. Hugging her knees,
Kaya sat beside her grandmother.

"I was looking for you, Granddaughter," Kautsa
said. "Where were you?" She rubbed her shoulders and
arms with the soft tips of the fir branches that covered
the floor.

"I went to see the puppies again," Kaya said.
Already she felt sweat running off her face and down
her back.

"How is the lone dog behaving now?" Kaya's grandmother asked, handing her a handful of the sweet-smelling fir to scrub herself.

"She likes me to visit her," Kaya murmured. Although her grandmother had given her permission to feed Lone Dog, Kaya knew she didn't really trust the dog. "Her pups are getting big and fat."

"Tawts," Kautsa said. "Soon she'll start to wean them. Then they'll join our dog pack—if the lone dog lets them."

Kaya leaned closer to her grandmother. "Sometimes Lone Dog seems to be talking to me with her eyes," she whispered. "Do you believe me?"

"Aa-heh!" Kautsa said right away. "I believe you. Animals talk to us in many, many ways."

"But I mean she really *speaks* to me, too," Kaya whispered even more softly.

Kautsa sat with her head bent, silently breathing in the cleansing steam. After a time, she said, "I'm thinking about my mother. When she was a girl, she received a wolf spirit, and after that she could talk with wolves. One day, when she was very old, a wolf trotted along the trail where she was picking berries.

The wolf was sad because her puppies had died. My mother was very sorry for the wolf. She asked the wolf if she could help her. The wolf told her that she was leaving the mountains, and refused help. But then she gave my mother the gift of her wolf power. That power made my mother even stronger."

"The wolf spoke to her?" Kaya asked. "Like Lone Dog speaks to me?"

"All creatures have wisdom to share with us," Kautsa said. "Soon you'll prepare for your vision quest, and I hope you'll receive a *wyakin* of your own. If you do, you must always listen closely to what it tells you."

"Aa-heh!" Kaya said. With all her heart, she hoped to be ready for her vision quest. Would she receive wolf power, as her great-grandmother had? As Kaya tried to imagine that, Eetsa pulled aside the deerskin covering the door and signaled everyone to leave the steamy lodge and plunge into the stream again.

"You're too old to quarrel like this!" Kaya said to the twins. "Listen to me and do as I say!" She held Wing Feather by one hand and Sparrow by the other. The little boys had been wrestling playfully on the hillside when their game suddenly became too rough.

Sparrow tried to pull his hand from her grasp.

Wing Feather scowled. "We lost most of our arrows," he said. "If you make us some more, I promise we won't fight over them."

"Aa-heh," Kaya said. "If you sit there quietly, I'll make more arrows for you." She sighed as she cut some straight twigs from an elderberry bush. Her little brothers were full of energy and full of tricks. Eetsa told Kaya to take care of them even more often now that she couldn't dig roots with the other girls and women.

But the twins didn't pay enough attention to Kaya's warnings. Kaya wished she could teach the boys to obey her as easily as Lone Dog had taught her pups. Usually it took the dog no more than a soft growl or a shake to bring her troublesome pups in line again.

Like the twins, the pups romped and wrestled and tugged and chased one another all day. But sometimes Lone Dog gave a special growl that meant, *Take cover!* Then they tumbled back into the den, where they were safe from bobcats, or an eagle hovering overhead. *She's taught her pups well,* Kaya thought as she finished cutting notches in the arrows.

"Here, boys," Kaya said. "I've made two arrows for each of you. You can go hunting again."

Wing Feather had fallen asleep on the soft grass, his hand tucked into his baby moccasin, which he always kept with him. He rolled onto his back and rubbed his eyes with it. "Katsee-yow-yow!" he said, reaching for the little arrows.

Kaya looked around for Sparrow. He'd been lying on his stomach by his brother, but now he was nowhere to be seen.

"Is that bothersome boy hiding from me again?" Kaya asked Wing Feather. "I have to find him. Do you know which way he might have gone?"

Wing Feather's lower lip stuck out. "He should have waited for me. I told him we couldn't visit the puppies without you, but he—"

Puppies! Kaya's pulse sped. She imagined Sparrow sneaking up on Lone Dog's den, determined to touch the pups. She didn't believe that Lone Dog would hurt the boy, but she couldn't be certain. She knew only that she had to get to her brother as fast as she could.

"Come on!" she said. She grabbed Wing Feather's hand and started running.

Kaya and her little brother rushed down the path alongside the stream. Then they turned and ran up the long, steep hillside. Lone Dog's den was on the far side of the hill, hidden from view by underbrush.

Kaya paused on the crest of the hill to look for Sparrow. In a moment, she saw him coming around the base of the hill below her. He was running as silently as a shadow, as he'd been taught. He was going to get to the den before she could. Would Lone Dog chase him away with a nip?

Kaya could barely make out the entrance of the den. Something dark moved there, but it didn't look like a dog. Then Kaya realized that a bear was digging at the opening of the den, trying to get at the hidden puppies! And, running uphill, Sparrow wouldn't be able to see the bear until he'd reached the clearing!

"Stay here!" Kaya commanded Wing Feather, and she took off racing for the den as fast as she could. But it was like running in a bad dream—her feet felt as if they were weighted with stones. She didn't shout for Sparrow to stay back because she didn't want to startle

the bear—if it turned on her little brother, it could kill
him with a single swipe of its sharp claws!

Then the bear heard Sparrow coming. It swung
around and lumbered away from the den, its huge head
swaying, its jaws wide. Just at that moment, Sparrow
burst into the clearing. He saw the bear and skidded
to a halt. Then he scrambled toward the den as if he
wanted to crawl into it with the puppies. But there
was no way for him to hide from the bear, which was
heading right for him!

A Sad Parting

 pale streak flew by Kaya and plunged down the hill toward the den—it was Lone Dog! She was barking ferociously with alarm, her teeth bared and her hackles raised. With a long leap, she hurled herself down at the bear. She snapped viciously at its heels and lunged at its flanks. The bear rose onto its hind legs, swatting at Lone Dog, trying to grab her with its claws. There was blood on Lone Dog's back and shoulders, but she kept up her fierce attack. She was determined to protect her pups—and Sparrow—even if it meant her life.

Kaya ran into the clearing. She yelled as loudly as she could, waving her arms over her head. The bear looked her way. It went down on all fours again and backed off a little, confused by the noise. Then it chose not to fight. As it turned away, Lone Dog continued to bite at its heels, moving it along until it had disappeared into the thick underbrush and was gone. Still barking, Lone Dog dashed back to the den and her puppies.

Kaya ran to Sparrow. Hugging himself, he crouched against the hillside. He was crying. Kaya threw her arms around her little brother and held him close.

Wing Feather came leaping down the slope. "I saw it all!" he called out as he came. "Lone Dog fought just like a wolf! She saved her puppies, and she saved Sparrow, too!"

"Aa-heh, you're safe now!" Kaya tipped up Sparrow's chin so she could look him in the eye. "But if it hadn't been for Lone Dog, you wouldn't have had a chance against that bear. You owe your life to a very brave dog."

A few days later, Kaya piled some deerskins onto a travois and hitched it to the gray horse. The gentle gray's hoof was healed, and she accepted the travois as if she'd always pulled one—Kaya's training had been good. As Kaya rode out to the dog den on the hillside, she considered her plan. Lone Dog had weaned her pups, and Kaya knew they were at an age when they should get accustomed to other dogs and to people, too. She thought that if she took the pups to the village with her, maybe she could lure Lone Dog to follow. She hoped Lone Dog would live by their tepee and be her special dog now.

The pups were prancing about in front of the den. Tatlo had a small bone in his mouth, and the other three pups were chasing after him, trying to get it. When his little sister managed to pry it away, Tatlo rolled her onto her back and buried his face in her neck, growling. She pawed at Tatlo's face. They seemed to be fighting, but their tails were wagging.

Lone Dog lay on the hillside above the den, her head resting on her paws. With the help of a poultice of *wapalwaapal* that Kaya had made, her wounds were healing well. When Kaya slid off the horse, Lone Dog got to her feet and stretched. Then she came to lean affectionately against Kaya's legs. Kaya scratched her back just above her tail. "Your pups are growing fast, aren't they?" Kaya said to her friend. "Now they can become part of our dog pack."

Lone Dog looked toward her pups wrestling for the bone, then back at Kaya. Would this solitary dog allow her pups to live among people?

"And I hope you'll come to live with me, too," Kaya said softly.

Lone Dog looked away. After a moment, she went back to the hillside and lay down again. She seemed to be thinking over what Kaya had said.

Kaya rounded up the puppies and put them into the makeshift nest on the travois. They curled up together, as if pleased to be going on a ride. Kaya mounted the horse and called, "Come, Lone Dog! Come!" Hoping that Lone Dog would follow, she began to ride slowly toward the path that led to the village. When she glanced over her shoulder, Lone Dog was trotting down the hillside to follow them.

But Kaya's worries were far from over. Everyone trusted Lone Dog since she'd saved Sparrow, but Kaya wasn't sure what Snow Paws would do when he saw Lone Dog approach the village. Would he still think she was a danger? In an all-out fight, he could injure or kill her. As Kaya rode toward the tepees, she watched warily for the big black dog.

Soon Snow Paws came barking loudly to confront Lone Dog. He took a stand near the tepees and set himself to defend the village.

Kautsa was making finger cakes with some other women. "Snow Paws, go!" she commanded the dog. "Go!" she repeated even more loudly. "Lone Dog belongs here now!"

Snow Paws stopped barking, but he approached Lone Dog slowly on stiff legs. Lone Dog stood perfectly still, her ears slightly back—she was in his territory now. He sniffed her, then allowed her to sniff him in return. When he walked back to the other dogs, Kaya knew he had accepted Lone Dog as one of the pack. Oh, she hoped Lone Dog would stay with her here in the village!

Kautsa was stringing dried roots and dried kouse cakes on hemp cord so they could be carried easily when it was time to travel again. Kaya worked at her grandmother's side, cutting the cord into even lengths and handing the pieces to her as she needed them.

The season for digging roots here was coming to

an end. Soon everyone would leave the Palouse Prairie and journey to the meadows to dig camas there. Kaya knew the camas plants were already in bloom, their deep blue flowers making the meadows look like vast, shimmering lakes. And soon it would be time for the spring salmon runs, too. Kaya loved to travel, but now she worried that Lone Dog might not follow her when they broke camp, although her pups had joined the dog pack.

Lone Dog didn't seem to be at ease around people or the other dogs. When Kaya was in the camp, Lone Dog stayed near her side. But when Kaya left the camp for wood or water, Lone Dog ran off by herself into the hills, sometimes staying away all night.

"Is something troubling you, Granddaughter?" Kautsa asked. She held out her hand for another piece of cord.

"Aa-heh," Kaya admitted. "Do you remember I told you that Lone Dog sometimes speaks to me?"

"What does Lone Dog tell you these days?" Kautsa asked.

"I think she's saying that she's going to leave us," Kaya said. "She's not meant to be a village dog."

Kautsa nodded. "It's true that she's different from our other dogs. Perhaps it's her nature to live alone."

"But I don't want her to leave me!" Kaya burst out. "I want her to be my dog always!"

Kautsa thought for a while. Then she picked up the ball of hemp cord and held it out to Kaya. "You could tie this rope around her neck so she couldn't run off. Have you thought of doing that?"

Kaya frowned in concentration. She tried to think what Swan Circling would do. "If I tied up Lone Dog, she'd be the same as a captive, wouldn't she?" she asked miserably. "The enemies from Buffalo Country tied me up every night. The rope kept me from running away, but I was desperate to escape. Lone Dog would feel the same way. I couldn't do that to her. I couldn't!"

Her grandmother put her warm hand on Kaya's shoulder. "Listen to me. I have something to tell you."

Kaya looked up at her grandmother, who was gazing at her with love and concern. "I know it will be hard for you to let Lone Dog go her own way," Kautsa said thoughtfully. "But, as you said yourself, someone who has been a captive understands the powerful need to be free. Can you respect what's best for her?"

Kaya bit her lip. She didn't want to imagine her life without Lone Dog in it.

On the morning the women began to pack up all their belongings for the journey to the camas meadows, Kaya went looking for Lone Dog. She hadn't seen the dog since the men had rounded up the horses the day before and brought them to camp to be loaded for the trip. Kaya looked all around the camp, calling her name. Where was she? Was she up there on the ridge? Kaya ran up to the top, then over the hill to the abandoned den on the far side. She saw the striped face of a badger that had taken over the empty den. But Lone Dog was nowhere to be seen.

Kaya remembered that sometimes Lone Dog had been gone for longer than this. But by the time the women had rolled up all the tule mats and stashed the tepee poles to be used the next year, Lone Dog was still missing.

Raven came by, leading some pack horses. "I hear your dog's run off," he said, but he didn't sound pleased about it.

"She isn't *my* dog," Kaya said, as firmly as she could. "She belongs to herself. Anyway, she might follow us later." But in her heart, Kaya knew that Lone Dog had gone on her way—alone—as she needed to be.

Don't cry! Kaya told herself. *Keep good thoughts!* But her throat was tight with tears.

As Kaya was helping the twins climb onto a travois, she felt a tug at the hem of her dress. It was Tatlo, pulling at her skirt and begging to play.

When Kaya ignored him, he began to sniff the bundles piled up near the horses. She heard him give his puppy growl, then saw him drag something from one of the bundles. With another growl, he started shaking what he'd found—it was Speaking Rain's doll!

"Tatlo, that's not a toy for you!" Kaya cried. "Bring that to me!" She knew if she chased him, he'd run away from her with the precious doll. So she sat on the ground to encourage him to come closer. He paused, his head cocked. Then he trotted to her and dropped the doll into her lap, his whole body wiggling as if he knew he'd done something good.

"Tawts, Tatlo!" Kaya said. She pushed the doll behind her and lifted the pup onto her lap. "Are you telling me you're going to help me find my sister someday?" she asked him.

Tatlo put his paws on her shoulders and looked at her with his amber eyes. Then he nipped at her braids and licked her cheek and her chin. Kaya couldn't help but laugh as the rough little tongue tickled her face.

"Jump down, now," Kaya told him. But instead of jumping down, Tatlo turned around and around until he'd curled up in her lap. As soon as he laid his head on Kaya's legs, he was asleep.

Kaya gently stroked the sleeping puppy. His muzzle was pale, like Lone Dog's, and his big paws meant he'd grow to be large, like her. "I think your mother sent you to be my dog now," Kaya whispered to him. "We have a long, long way to travel, and I'll be very glad to have you with me."

The Sound of the Falls

ong before Kaya could see the waterfalls on the river ahead, she began to hear their voices. She and her family were riding over hot, dry plains, so the murmur of running water was a sweet promise. But as they rode closer to the river, that murmur grew into a powerful song, like many men drumming. When the riders crested the last hill and looked down at the shining river, Kaya saw the falls plunging over black cliffs. Even at this distance the falls roared like thunder. The earth seemed to tremble.

Wing Feather was seated behind Kaya on the chestnut horse. He held her tightly around the waist. "Is that a monster roaring?" he asked in a small voice.

Kaya patted his leg. "That's the sound of the falls you hear," she said. "Remember when we stayed here last summer? Remember how you and Sparrow played all day with your cousins, and there were games and races every night? And remember how many salmon gave themselves to all the fishermen?"

Wing Feather only hugged her more tightly, one hand tucked into his baby moccasin. Kaya knew he was trying to be strong, but the roar of Celilo Falls frightened many children.

"The water sounds angry!" Sparrow said. He was riding behind Brown Deer.

"But the river's our friend, and you'll soon get used to its roar," Brown Deer said. Her voice was calm, but her cheeks were flushed with excitement. Kaya knew her sister was eager to meet family and friends here at the falls. Brown Deer would also meet Cut Cheek again, whom she hoped to marry.

Kaya's father, who rode ahead, signaled for everyone to halt before beginning the steep descent from the bluffs into the valley. He and other men and women dismounted and began checking the heavy packs to make sure they were tied tightly and wouldn't slip and injure a horse or rider.

Kaya dismounted and gazed down at the vast river

valley. Stony islands clustered in the river, white water sweeping around them. Kaya saw large horse herds grazing on the flatlands. Many fishing platforms of sticks lashed together had been built out over the water. Hundreds of tepees and lodges lined both shores as far upstream and downstream as she could see. The villages were those of many different peoples—some who lived on the river all year and others who visited from the plains, the mountains, and the ocean to fish and trade. Kaya's band, and many other bands of Nimíipuu, were joining them for the yearly return of salmon up the Big River.

Kaya shaded her eyes and peered at the mist that rose like thick smoke from the waterfalls. She saw bright rainbows arching low over the falls, and her heart lifted. Rainbows were good signs. She hoped to meet up with her friend Two Hawks here at the falls. He'd said that when they met again, he might have good news of Speaking Rain.

But Kaya knew that Two Hawks might be bringing bad news instead. He might have learned that Speaking Rain had been abandoned by their captors—or injured, or lost. For how could a blind girl get along without someone to care for her?

As if Tatlo sensed Kaya's troubled thoughts, the pup bounded up to her, his pink tongue hanging out. He was growing fast, and his legs were getting long. Kaya bent and put her face against his soft ear. "You'll help me find my sister, won't you?" she whispered to him. He licked her hand, his tail wagging in circles, as if he were saying, *I'll try.*

Kaya's grandmother climbed off her horse and began adjusting the travois on a pack horse. When Kautsa saw the twins' worried frowns, her lined face softened. "Aa-heh, the falls are hissing and raging, boys," she said, "but that's because they're so steep and so wide. Don't you remember how Coyote made them for us?" She turned to Kaya. "Would you comfort your brothers with that story while I fix this travois?"

"Aa-heh," Kaya said quickly. Each day she reminded herself to do her very best. She wanted to be trustworthy like her friend Swan Circling.

Wing Feather and Sparrow slid off the horses. "Tell about Coyote!" Sparrow begged her.

"Tell about his tricks!" Wing Feather added. Everyone loved stories about Coyote, who was always playing tricks and teaching lessons at the same time.

Kaya sat with the twins on a travois, and Tatlo, panting, lay down in the shade at their feet. "One day Coyote was coming up the river," she began. "And in those long-ago days the river was calm, because the River People had dammed it up—they wanted to keep all the salmon for themselves. Coyote was hot and tired, like we are, and he decided to swim in the cool water. He swam around until he saw five beautiful river girls on the shore. He saw a chance to play a trick on the River People, so he turned himself into a baby and came floating over the water toward the girls."

"I remember what Coyote did then!" Wing Feather cried. "He bawled like a baby—*Wah! Wah!*—to get the girls' attention!"

"Aa-heh," Kaya said. "He cried, and the girls quickly swam out to pull him from the water. 'What a precious baby!' they said. But the youngest sister wasn't fooled. 'Watch out!' she said. 'That's no baby. That's Coyote!' The baby put out his lower lip as if he was about to cry again. 'Don't tease him,' the other girls said. 'Let's take him home with us.'

"The girls fed the baby and took care of him, and

he grew fast. One day he spilled a cup of water. 'Get me more water!' he demanded. The youngest sister, who still didn't trust the baby, said, 'Let's make him get water himself.' So the baby began to crawl toward the river. When he was out of sight, he jumped up and ran. 'He certainly moves fast!' one of the girls said. The youngest sister said, 'That's because he's Coyote!'"

"I know what happened next!" Sparrow cried. "Coyote broke down the fish dam that the River People had made!"

"Aa-heh, Coyote swam up to their fish dam and tore it down, pulling out all the stones so the water rushed free over the falls," Kaya continued. "He jumped up and down on the stones and shouted gleefully, 'Look, your fish dam is broken!' The girls saw that it was so. The youngest sister said, 'I told you he was Coyote!'

"Coyote said to them, 'You selfishly kept all the salmon behind your dam. But now the salmon will be able to swim upstream to spawn. People will be happy because they can catch the fish, and they'll thank me for giving them food.' And that's how Celilo Falls came to be, and why salmon can swim up all the rivers and streams now," Kaya finished.

"Did Coyote really make those waterfalls?"
Sparrow asked, pointing at the water rushing over
black stones. Because he was thinking about the story,
he was no longer frightened.

"You can see for yourself that the fish dam's not
there anymore," Kaya said with a smile. "And who else
but Coyote could have knocked it down so that the
salmon could swim upstream?"

She scratched Tatlo behind his ears and gazed at
the distant hills across the river. Would Two Hawks
and his people soon be riding over those hills? Would
she be strong no matter what news he brought of
Speaking Rain? And what of her beloved horse—
would she discover Steps High in one of the many
horse herds here at the falls?

"Katsee-yow-yow for telling the story," Kautsa said.
"Come along now. We're ready to move on."

After Kaya and the others greeted friends and
relatives, the women set up their tepees and unpacked
their goods. Then Eetsa gave Kaya permission to join
the other girls, all of whom were like cousins to her.

Some girls had gathered on a flat stretch of ground to play a stickball game called Shinny. They'd formed two teams and were chasing a rawhide ball, hitting it to each other with curved sticks. As Kaya walked up, several of the girls waved to her.

"Play on our side, Kaya!" Little Fawn called to her. "You're a fast runner!"

"Play on our side!" Rabbit called. "Magpies fly fast!"

Magpie, again! As Kaya picked up a shinny stick, she tried to shrug off that awful nickname. And as soon as she was running down the field with the others, she forgot about everything except the game. The girls batted the ball and passed it to each other, trying to hit it between two branches stuck in the ground at each end of the playing field. Some dogs, barking wildly, ran along with them.

Little Fawn knocked the ball to Kaya, and she raced down the field with it, Tatlo right at her heels. But when other girls charged after Kaya, Tatlo got caught in the middle of the action. Someone stepped on his paw, and, with a yelp, he tumbled head over heels. Kaya stopped playing and led her pup to the sidelines.

Rabbit was there, tying her moccasins more tightly.

"Tawts may-we, cousin!" she greeted Kaya.

"Tawts may-we! Have you been here at the river long?" Kaya stroked Tatlo's ears as she caught her breath.

"Not long," Rabbit said. "Only for two sleeps."

"I want to find Two Hawks," Kaya said. "Have you seen him?"

"Raven went looking for him yesterday," Rabbit said. "He told us that no Salish people have come here yet. They don't always make the long journey, you know."

"I know," Kaya admitted. Two Hawks had given his promise, but his people might have made different plans. Her heart sank when she thought that he might not be able to bring her news of Speaking Rain after all.

"Your pup runs fast," Rabbit said, holding out her hand for Tatlo to sniff. "But I think his rear legs run faster than his front legs!"

"Aa-heh," Kaya said. "I'm going to tie him by our tepee so he won't get trampled."

"Come back quickly!" Rabbit called after her.

When Kaya approached her tepee, an elderly, gray-haired woman Kaya didn't recognize was carrying her belongings inside. Brown Deer knelt by a travois, untying more rolls of tule mats. She beckoned for Kaya to come close. "Cut Cheek's parents have sent one of his aunts to live with us for a while," she said in a low voice. "Crane Song's here to make sure I'm a strong worker and will make a good wife for Cut Cheek." She looked pleased, but she seemed nervous as well.

"Everyone knows you're a strong worker!" Kaya assured her sister, who was so dutiful and so good.

Brown Deer shook her head. "A woman has to prove her worth," she said softly.

"You'll be a fine wife for Cut Cheek. His aunt will see that right away," Kaya insisted. She tied one end of a piece of cord around Tatlo's neck and the other end to one of the tepee stakes.

Brown Deer frowned. "Tie Tatlo farther away, will you? Sometimes he chews on the tepee coverings, and I won't have time to look after him."

Kaya led Tatlo to a stack of tepee poles and tied him there. He sat with his ears drooping, whining as if he were being punished.

"Katsee-yow-yow, Kaya," Brown Deer said gratefully. She picked up the mats and hurried into the tepee, where Crane Song waited for her.

Kaya patted Tatlo on his rump. "Don't whine,"
she told him. "I'll be back for you soon."

At the beginning of each new run of salmon, everyone honored and thanked the fish with a feast. Kautsa
and the other women built big, slow-burning fires to
roast the salmon. While the fish cooked under the
open sky, the women spread rows of tule mats down
the center of a lodge large enough to seat all their
family and friends. Kaya stood with the other girls and
women across from the men and boys while her grandfather led them in prayer.

"Hun-ya-wat made this earth," Pi-lah-ka said. "He
made all living things on the earth, in the water, and in
the sky. He made Nimíipuu and all peoples. He created
food for all His creatures. We respect and give thanks
for His creations."

All the people took a sip of water to purify their
bodies before they accepted the gifts from the Creator.
After everyone had taken a sip of the cold river water,
each person took a tiny bite of salmon, giving thanks

before beginning the rest of the meal.

The men and boys served the roasted meat they'd
provided. The women and girls brought forward the
foods they'd gathered. With the others, Kaya placed
bowls filled with roots and berries on the mats. Then
the women brought large wooden bowls of the cooked
salmon into the lodge.

Kaya watched Brown Deer moving quickly and
quietly along the mats. It was a great honor to feed
the others, and Brown Deer kept her eyes downcast,
even when she offered Cut Cheek a bowl. But her face
reddened slightly when he took it from her.

*Surely Crane Song will see what a fine woman Brown
Deer is,* Kaya thought. And soon Cut Cheek would
prove his worth by fishing well and bravely with the
other men. If their parents approved, the couple could
marry in the autumn.

That thought made Kaya's heart glad—and also sad.
She wanted Brown Deer to marry Cut Cheek, but she
was sad to think of her sister leaving their family. She'd
lost one sister when she'd had to leave Speaking Rain
with the enemies. Now she felt she might be losing her
other sister as well.

Dangerous Crossing!

CHAPTER 7

When Kaya followed her mother and the other women to the riverbank the next morning, the men and boys were already fishing. Some spearfished from rocky outcroppings along the shore. Others stood on sturdy poles lashed together to make platforms built out over the falls. They held their long-handled dip nets down into the crashing waters. When a salmon leaped into a dip net, the force of the current closed the net around it. But it took great strength to lift a large, struggling fish, and if a man was pulled into the rushing water, he could be swept over the falls and drowned. For safety, the men tied lines around their waists and secured the lines to rocks. Kaya shivered as she saw Toe-ta and the others leaning over the raging waters.

The men's work was difficult and dangerous, but

the women and girls worked hard, too. All day Kaya helped carry the heavy salmon the men caught to the women who cleaned the fish and sliced them into thin strips. Other women hung the strips on racks, to be dried by the sun and wind. By the end of the day, Kaya's hands, arms, and back ached.

As Kaya walked with Kautsa to their village upstream above the falls, she wiped her eyes with a handful of soft grass. "The wind makes my eyes sting," she said.

"Aa-heh," Kautsa said, wiping her own eyes. "The wind blowing up the gorge is a powerful force! But it's another gift from Hun-ya-wat. With so much wind, fish dry very quickly. There's no need to build drying fires here at the falls."

Kaya looked back down the valley at the villages that crowded the shore. "I've been watching for Salish people to arrive," she said. "Two Hawks might come with them."

"They could be on the other side of the river," Kautsa said. "Two women came across today in a canoe to trade with us. I don't speak their language, but Crane Song knows it. The traders told her that newcomers from the north were putting up tepees over there."

Kaya felt a shiver of hope. "Did they say anything about a blind girl?"

"About our Speaking Rain?" Kautsa asked. "If they had, I'd have taken a canoe to see for myself! But they said only that the newcomers had hide-covered tepees, not like ours."

"Two Hawks's people have hide tepees!" Kaya said. "Couldn't I cross the river with the traders and see who the newcomers are? I could cross back later with some fishermen."

Kautsa looked kindly into Kaya's eyes. "I know you won't be satisfied until you see for yourself," she said. "The traders tied their canoe upstream. Surely they'll have room for you. Take them some finger cakes as a gift."

Kaya ran to their camping place, where Brown Deer was sweeping the ground with a broom of sage branches. Her older sister looked tired and unhappy.

"Is something wrong?" Kaya asked.

"I think something's wrong with *me*," Brown Deer admitted. "I'm doing my very best to please Crane Song.

I was the first one to waken, long before first light. I brought fresh water and built up the fire before she'd even stirred. Still, all she did was frown and shake her head as though I'm not working hard enough."

"You've always been hardworking and respectful," Kaya insisted. "And you're strong and good, too."

"I'm trying my very best," Brown Deer said. "I don't think my best is good enough for Crane Song."

"But of all the girls, Cut Cheek chose you!" Kaya said, her face hot with feeling. "And you chose him, too! That means more than anything, doesn't it?"

"It does to us," Brown Deer said. "But if Crane Song isn't convinced I'll make a good wife, Cut Cheek's family won't approve of our marriage."

Kaya couldn't believe what she was hearing. All her life she'd admired her older sister, and she feared she would never be as steady or as strong as Brown Deer. "What does Kautsa say about this?" she asked.

"Kautsa says these things take time," Brown Deer said. "She says to be patient, that Crane Song might seem hard-hearted, but she's fair. What do you think, Kaya?"

"I think Kautsa is wise in all things," Kaya said,

adding, "You can trust her judgment."

"I hope so," Brown Deer said. "Everything depends on Crane Song's good opinion of me." She set aside the broom and got her knife and workbag. "I've finished cleaning here," she said. "Now I have to join her. Wish me well, Sister." Walking fast, she took the path toward where the women were cutting up salmon and spreading the strips onto drying racks.

Kaya ran into their tepee and put a handful of kouse cakes into the bag she wore on her belt. Then she had an idea. She took Speaking Rain's doll from her pack and tucked it into her belt. If, somehow, she found her sister, she wanted to put the beloved doll into her arms—a sign that she'd never lost hope they'd be together again.

Tatlo was sleeping in the shade beside the tepee. When Kaya came out with the doll, she crouched and he jumped up and licked her chin. Then he sniffed the doll and licked it, too.

"Do you want to come with me?" Kaya asked. Tatlo barked twice, as if saying *Aa-heh!* He ran ahead as she raced up the shore to where two women were putting bundles into a dugout cedar canoe.

Kaya threw the elder woman the words, *May I cross the river with you?*

With her hands, the elder woman said, *Come with us.*

Gratefully, Kaya gave her the kouse cakes and climbed into the canoe, with Tatlo jumping in right behind.

The young woman knelt in the prow of the canoe, and the elder woman sat in the stern. The elder woman expertly guided the canoe away from shore. Soon they were paddling across a place where the water was shallower and quieter than the rest of the river. This was a prized fishing place because it was easy to see salmon in the clear, smoothly running water. A fisherman could slip his net over a large fish, just like roping a horse.

Kaya saw the boys Raven and Fox Tail fishing together on a little island just downstream. They'd tied their safety lines around the same rock, and they were taking turns using a big dip net. As Kaya watched, Raven dragged up the net with a large salmon twisting in it. Fox Tail helped him hold the long, heavy pole until they got the netted fish onto the rocks. Raven took his fish club and killed the salmon with a single blow. Kaya could see it was a good catch.

The many fish leaping and splashing around the canoe excited Tatlo. He put his feet up on the side and barked at them. "Get down!" Kaya said. "Down!" She grabbed the big pup by the scruff of his neck and tried to make him sit. But Tatlo was too excited to sit. When a salmon jumped right next to the canoe, he lunged and snapped at it—and toppled out of the canoe into the river! The surging current caught him and swept him downstream.

"Help my dog!" Kaya cried. The wind whipped her braids across her face and tore away her words. She watched in horror as Tatlo struggled to swim in the churning river. His paws thrashed the water, and his amber eyes looked about wildly. Each time he came up for air, the current dragged him under again. Surely he'd be swept down to the falls and killed on the rocks below!

The elder woman turned the canoe downstream, and the young woman paddled hard and fast. But Kaya knew there was no way they could catch up to Tatlo. Already the current had carried him downstream almost to the island.

Then she saw Raven looking their way. He quickly

thrust the dip net back into the river. Fox Tail leaned
out and peered down into the wild water. Then, with a
sweep, Raven raised the net with something in it. Fox
Tail grabbed the handle, too, and steadied the heavy
weight against his body as he helped lift the net. It took
a long moment for Kaya to realize that it was Tatlo they
lifted out of the swirling water!

The elder woman guided the canoe toward the
island. By the time they beached on the stones, the boys
had Tatlo out of the net and onto his feet. The pup was
coughing water and shaking it from his coat. His legs
were wobbly, but he managed to wag his tail when
Kaya scrambled from the canoe and knelt by him,
pressing her face against his drenched head.

"The current carried him right to us!" Raven yelled
over the river noise.

Then Fox Tail leaned toward Kaya with a sly grin.
He put his mouth near her ear and shouted, "Magpies
don't know how to take care of dogs!"

That awful nickname again! *But he's right*, she
thought. *I didn't take care of Tatlo. I should have held him
every moment. It's my fault he fell in.* Instead of hanging her head, she looked Fox Tail right in the eye and

flapped her arms like a magpie. They both started laughing.

"Katsee-yow-yow!" she shouted so the boys could hear her thanks. With Tatlo shivering against her legs, she climbed back into the canoe so that they could continue on to the opposite shore.

Kaya made her way through the many villages crowded along the shore. She saw people from the coast trading dried shellfish, shell beads, cedar-root baskets, and canoes. People from the south had brought bowls of black stone and baskets of water-lily seeds to trade. And the people who lived in the midlands, like Kaya's people, traded elk and buffalo robes, kouse and camas cakes, and horses. But Kaya wasn't interested in the trading. She had only one thing on her mind—finding the newcomers from the north.

Tatlo stayed right by her side, his nose twitching at all the new scents around them. If any of the dogs that roamed about came too close to Kaya, a growl rose in his throat and his ears went back. He was such a loyal friend—how terrible if he had drowned because she hadn't kept him in the canoe! "I'll take better care of you," she said, patting his shoulder.

Kaya's ears buzzed with all the different languages she heard. From time to time she stopped where women were cooking and threw them the words, *Where are the newcomers camped?* Always they pointed east, so she kept walking upstream. At last she saw several hide-covered tepees ringed in a small circle. Women were building fires and carrying bundles into the tepees. Could these be Two Hawks's people? She ran, with Tatlo loping at her side.

A young woman was unloading deerskin bags from a travois. Kaya threw her the words, *What tribe are you?*

The young woman cocked her head and studied Kaya closely. She signed, *I am Salish. What tribe are you?*

Kaya swept her hand from her ear down across her chin, the sign for Nimíipuu. *Is Two Hawks with you?* she signed. *He wintered with our people.*

Two Hawks told us about you, the young woman signed. *Right now he's fishing with the men.* She motioned for Kaya to follow her to where women were putting up another tepee.

A white-haired woman with a bent back was

smoothing the elk-skin tepee covering. A round-faced younger woman was pounding tepee stakes into the ground. As Kaya and the Salish woman approached these women, Tatlo sniffed the air a moment, then bounded away and began ranging back and forth between the tepees. "Tatlo! Come!" Kaya called, wanting to keep him close to her. When he didn't come, she ran after him.

Horses grazed near the tepees. Tatlo ran between them, his tail wagging, and headed for some small pines. Kaya followed. She saw a baby in a *tee-kas* propped against one of the pines. Tatlo was sniffing the girl who sat tending the baby. The girl's back was to Kaya, who was so intent on catching her pup that she didn't realize until she was only a few steps away that the girl was Speaking Rain!

"Sister! My sister!" Kaya cried. She felt tears sting her eyes as she went to her knees in front of Speaking Rain and seized her hand. "You're alive!"

"Kaya?" Speaking Rain hesitantly touched Kaya's face, then threw her arms around her shoulders. "Aa-heh, I'm alive! How did you find me?"

"I didn't find you," Kaya said. "My dog did! Tatlo

knows your scent from your doll." She took the doll from her belt and placed it in Speaking Rain's lap. "I mended it for you and kept it safe. I knew we'd be together again!"

Speaking Rain clutched her doll to her chest, her smile shining like sun on the water. "Katsee-yow-yow," she said softly. "I prayed for you every day."

"And I prayed for you," Kaya said. As she spoke, she looked closely at her sister. When Kaya had last seen her, Speaking Rain had been thin and frail and dirty. Now she wore a fine buckskin dress decorated with many beads and elks' teeth. Her cheeks were round, and her glossy hair was sleekly braided and tied with abalone-shell ties. She wore a pretty necklace of white clamshell beads. "Two Hawks's people have been good to you, haven't they?" Kaya said.

"Aa-heh, they've been very good to me," Speaking Rain said.

Tatlo was gazing intently up at Speaking Rain, as though he recognized her. Kaya placed her sister's hand on his head. "Tatlo likes you. He's a smart dog, but even if he hadn't sniffed you out, I'd have found you."

"If Two Hawks didn't find you first!" Speaking Rain

said. "He told me he was going to cross the river to look for you at sunup."

Kaya took a deep breath. "Brown Deer will be so excited to see you! Our parents will be so glad to have you with us again!"

Speaking Rain's face sobered. "I have so much to tell you," she said. "But I smell rain in the air, and don't you hear the wind rising? A storm is coming, and I should take the baby inside. Help me, and we'll talk more later."

Stranded by the Storm

aya remembered that storms here on the Big River were often fierce ones. She picked up the baby and hurried with Speaking Rain toward the women, where the baby's mother took him and carried him into her tepee. The wind quickly grew wilder. As the sky blackened, other women rushed to bring their belongings and coals for the fires inside. Tatlo whined, wanting to follow Kaya, then huddled up with the other dogs, his head buried in his tail.

The white-haired woman led the girls to her tepee. When they were inside, she fastened the tepee flaps securely against the gusts. The woman was plump-cheeked and very old, her shoulders bent as if she were carrying a heavy load. She unrolled an elk hide and motioned for Kaya to sit on it. Then she led Speaking

Rain to the hide, and spoke quietly with her. Kaya was surprised to realize that Speaking Rain spoke Salish now.

"I told White Braids that you're my sister," Speaking Rain said to Kaya. "She's the one who found me and saved my life."

Thank you for saving my sister! Kaya signed to White Braids.

You are welcome here with us, White Braids signed to Kaya. Then she poured water from a rawhide bag into a cooking basket, and set about heating stones in the fire so that she could cook with them.

Kaya leaned close to Speaking Rain. "Tell me what happened after I escaped and left you behind," Kaya urged her. "Many times I've thought how hard it must have been for you. I should never have gone!"

"But I wanted you to go!" Speaking Rain insisted. She held her doll tightly. "I *couldn't* have kept up with you. Two Hawks told us how difficult your journey was."

Pelting rain began to drive against the tepee covering. "This storm reminds me of the night I escaped," Kaya said. "Was Otter Woman angry when she discovered I was gone? Did she whip you for helping me get away?"

"She was angry, but she didn't whip me," Speaking Rain said. "They were all hurrying to pack up and break camp. They wanted to get back to their own country before snow stranded them."

"Somehow you got away from them, too," Kaya said. "Or did they abandon you?"

Speaking Rain put her hand on Kaya's arm. "I don't know what happened, Sister. I found my way to the river to drink and wash. When I came back, everyone was gone. Maybe in their rush they forgot about me. I was alone."

"My poor sister!" Kaya breathed. "What did you do?"

"I tried to stay calm," Speaking Rain said. "I needed a place to sleep, to hide. I crawled through the thicket near the river until I found grass trampled where deer had bedded down. Low branches sheltered the nest. I decided to stay there. Even if I could have found a trail, I'd never have been able to follow it."

"Did you have any food?" Kaya asked.

"They'd taken all the food," Speaking Rain said.

"I tried to eat grass, but I couldn't keep it down. After a few sleeps, I was so weak that I could scarcely walk. And the nights grew colder and colder."

As Kaya listened to her sister's story, her heart hurt in her chest. "You must have been frightened," she said softly.

"I knew I would die, so I tried to make my spirit strong," Speaking Rain said. "But I drifted in and out of swirling dreams—awake, asleep? I didn't know anymore. Then I heard steps in the grass, steady ones—not a deer browsing. Someone was walking nearby. I moaned. The steps came closer, and then I felt a touch on my cheek."

"White Braids found you there?" Kaya said.

"Aa-heh," Speaking Rain said. "She was with a small group returning north. She'd come to the river to get driftwood for a fire."

"What happened after she found you?" Kaya asked.

"For a long time I was sick—coughing, choking," Speaking Rain said. "Each breath burned, and my face flamed. White Braids brewed wapalwaapal for my fever. Every day she carried me into a sweat lodge and bathed me. She fed me broth, then mush. She treated me as if I were her own child, and slowly I got stronger. When the digging season came, I was able to travel with her to the root fields. That's where Two Hawks and his family found me."

A sudden gust of wind forced smoke back inside the tepee. Squinting, White Braids fanned the smoke away from Speaking Rain, then went back to tending the fire. When the stones were hot, she dropped them into the basket of water and added pieces of salmon to boil.

"When White Braids was a young woman, she had a daughter," Speaking Rain said. "But her little girl died. White Braids says that now she has a second daughter—me. I sleep by her side and warm her. When her shoulders ache, I rub them. I carry bundles of firewood for her. She trades the hemp cord I make for hides and other things we need."

"You've cared for White Braids, just as she's cared for you," Kaya said. "Who will help her now that we've found you again?"

Speaking Rain pressed her fist to her lips. Then she took Kaya's hand in hers. "Listen to me," she said slowly, as if she'd thought through carefully what she wanted to say. "It's true that White Braids brought me here to join my family again. But, Kaya, when she saved my life, I made a vow that I'd never, ever leave her. I can't break that vow. I can never live with you again."

Kaya couldn't make sense of what she heard. Speaking Rain was back, she was safe—but she could never live with them again? "Why do you say that?" Her voice trembled with disbelief. "Eetsa and Toe-ta have been so sad! Brown Deer missed you terribly, and so did the twins. You're my sister! You must come back to us!"

Speaking Rain leaned closer and squeezed Kaya's hand harder. "Please, try to understand," she said. "When White Braids gave me back my life, I vowed I'd repay her. It was a solemn vow, Sister, and I won't break it. I know in my heart this is right."

Kaya stared at her sister's serious face. She didn't believe what she was hearing—no, she *couldn't* believe that she had found her sister only to lose her again! "Surely White Braids won't let you give up your family," Kaya said. "She lost her own daughter—she knows how sad your mother would be to lose you."

"I haven't told her yet that I'll never leave her,"

Speaking Rain admitted. "But I'm sure she'll respect my vow."

White Braids took the fish from the cooking basket with tongs and divided it into two bowls made of horn. She placed one bowl in Speaking Rain's hands and gave the other one to Kaya.

Kaya tried to eat the delicious food, but her mouth was so dry, she couldn't swallow. Her thoughts whirled like smoke in the wind. She wanted her sister back, but how could she convince Speaking Rain that it was best to be with her own family? And was it right to urge her sister to break her solemn vow?

Someone was at the doorway. White Braids unfastened the flaps and pulled them aside. It was Two Hawks. In a burst of rain he came, drenched, into the tepee, and he started when he saw Kaya. "Tawts, you're here!" he said. "You see, I did what I promised. I found your sister!"

"Aa-heh, you did as you said." Kaya was more grateful than she could say, and she was proud of him, too.

A powerful-looking man followed Two Hawks inside. He and the boy dried and warmed themselves with deer hides. Then, because Two Hawks could speak both languages, he acted as an interpreter. He told Kaya that the man was his father and that his mother had stayed behind in their own country. Then he told his father that Kaya was the girl who had fled with him over the Buffalo Trail.

Two Hawks's father put his hand on Kaya's shoulder. With Two Hawks interpreting, he told her he was grateful to her and her people. He wanted to greet her parents and unite them with their lost daughter again.

As Kaya listened, she thought, *They don't know Speaking Rain has decided not to come back to us. Though she sounds so sure, maybe she has her own doubts.*

Again Kaya thanked Two Hawks and his father. Then she asked if they'd seen her horse in any of their herds.

"No one has seen your horse yet," Two Hawks said. "But someone will have Nimíipuu horses—and yours. Don't give up hope."

"I'll try to keep hoping," Kaya said, keeping her voice steady. But could she?

Two Hawks's father spoke to him again.

"My father says you must stay with us tonight,"
Two Hawks told Kaya. "No one can take a canoe across
the river in a storm like this. When it's over, my father
will find some fishermen to take you to the other side."

Kaya didn't want to stay—she wanted to take her
sister back to her own people. Once Speaking Rain was
with them, she'd realize that it was right. But Kaya had
no choice.

White Braids served the men the food she'd
prepared, then sat down beside Speaking Rain. From
time to time she removed a small bone from Speaking
Rain's bowl of fish, or gave her more mashed berries.

After their meal, White Braids took out the fishing
net she was mending and gave Speaking Rain
shredded hemp to make cord. For a while they
worked quietly. Speaking Rain kept an even tension
on the strands of hemp as she rolled them together into
a long cord. Kaya marveled at how expert Speaking
Rain had become—her cord was smooth and strong.
Praising her work, White Braids patted her shoulder.

As Kaya watched them work, her own feelings
were as tightly twisted as the cord. She saw that her
sister wasn't just helping White Braids—the old woman

relied on her now in a way that Kaya and her family never had. It came to her that a part of Speaking Rain was already gone from them—and this time Kaya was the one to be left behind.

Tee-tew! Was that a birdcall? Glad to be distracted from her painful thoughts, Kaya looked over her shoulder. Two Hawks had taken a flute from his bag and had played those sweet notes on it. Looking pleased with himself, he held out the flute for Kaya to examine. This flute was longer and more finely crafted than the first one he'd made. And when he put it to his lips, he could play a melody.

They all listened to Two Hawks play the soft, beautiful song. Then his father laughed and said something to White Braids that made her laugh, too.

"What did he say?" Kaya asked her sister.

Speaking Rain leaned close. "He said that when he was young, he could play love songs well because he got so much practice!" she whispered with a smile. "He says that soon Two Hawks will be old enough to serenade the girls as he once did."

Kaya studied her friend. He was no longer the angry, stubborn, skinny boy who'd crossed the Buffalo

Trail with her. He was taller, his shoulders were broader, and his dark eyes were clear and bright. She realized with surprise that someday he would be a handsome young man. She wanted to tell him that she liked the tune he played, but suddenly she was shy. Instead, she took Speaking Rain's doll and with her finger showed her sister where she'd mended it.

Outside the tepee the storm howled, but inside it was dry and warm. When it was time to sleep, White Braids spread deer hides on both sides of the fire. Two Hawks and his father lay down on one side. On the other side, Speaking Rain lay on her bed of hides next to the old woman's. "Here's a place for you beside me," she said to Kaya, as though everything were just as it had always been. *Except that everything's different!* Kaya thought.

Kaya lay down and tried to sleep, but she was troubled and restless. She felt the familiar warmth of her sister's shoulder against her own, but in her heart she was cold and lonely. *Creator, spare my life from accidents, illness, and loneliness,* Kaya prayed silently. *Help me to face life with a strong will and without fear of man or beast—or change.*

A New Path

y the time Kaya and Tatlo were taken across the river the next morning, everyone was already at work. Kaya found her mother kneeling on a smooth rock, cutting the head off a large salmon and taking out the entrails, which she put into a basket to take to the trash heap. Kaya knelt beside her and used her hands to speak over the roar of the falls. *Speaking Rain is alive! She's over there!* Kaya pointed at the opposite shore.

Eetsa sat back on her heels, and her eyes filled with tears. It was a long moment before she could answer. *We'll cross the river tonight and bring her back,* she signed. *Go tell your grandmother!* She pointed toward the workplaces on the hillside.

Kaya found Kautsa on an upland rise, spreading salmon eggs to dry on tule mats. Here the smell of fish was especially strong. Attracted by it, bald eagles and condors circled overhead, riding the winds. The roar of the falls wasn't so loud on this side of the rise, and Kaya didn't have to shout to tell her grandmother about Speaking Rain.

Kautsa clasped Kaya's hand when she heard that Speaking Rain was alive. "I've hoped and prayed to hear this!" she said. "Tell me what happened to her after you two were separated."

Careful not to leave out anything, Kaya told all that had happened to her sister and about her life now with White Braids.

When Kaya was through, Kautsa handed her a basket of salmon eggs. "Hold this while I spread these eggs. When they're dry, you can have some for yourself to trade. Maybe you can get some beads, or a shell to hold them while you're working."

Kaya knelt in silence by her grandmother for a little while. Then she said, "Speaking Rain's different now, Kautsa."

"Do you mean she's grown?" Kautsa asked.

"She's a little taller, that's true, and her face is rounder," Kaya said. "But she's grown inside. She seems older. I always looked out for her. Now she doesn't seem to need my help anymore."

"If she can't see, she'll always need some help," Kautsa said. "That hasn't changed, has it?"

"She's still blind in her eyes," Kaya said. "But her heart sees things clearly."

"Everything you're telling me is good news, but you look troubled," Kautsa said. "Didn't you sleep well, Granddaughter?"

Kaya bit her lip. "I stared at the fire all night," she admitted. "But that's not what troubles me. Speaking Rain told me about an important vow she made, one she won't break, no matter what."

"A vow she refuses to break?" Kautsa asked. "Her spirit is strong, then. All that she's been through has made her that way. What was her vow?"

"She vowed she would never leave the woman who saved her life!" Kaya blurted out. "Because of that, she can't live with us anymore!"

Kautsa looked at Kaya. "Your sister is strong. But listen to me, Granddaughter, you have strength, too."

"Do you mean the strength I needed to escape from the enemies?" Kaya asked.

"Not exactly," Kautsa said. "I mean you have the strength to make hard choices."

"Are you telling me I should let Speaking Rain go?" Kaya asked.

"I'm not telling you that at all," Kautsa said. "You wanted your sister to live. Don't you want her to have the life she chooses?"

"But I want her to choose to live with me!" Kaya said. "With us! I would miss her so. You'd miss her, too, Kautsa!"

"Aa-heh, I would miss her very much," Kautsa admitted. Her face was grave, and she looked sad. "Remember how you wanted Lone Dog to stay with you? But it wasn't her nature to do that. Perhaps now Speaking Rain must follow her own path—just as you must follow yours."

The heat shimmering up from the stones and the smell of the fish made Kaya dizzy. She swayed, and Kautsa clasped her shoulder, then handed her the water basket so that she could drink. "I know you love your sister," Kautsa said gently. "You love your parents, and all your grandparents, and Brown Deer, and the twins—and others. You love many people.

So does Speaking Rain. If she loves and respects two mothers now, she has her own hard choice to make. Do you understand me?"

Kaya wiped her lips on her wrist. "Aa-heh," she murmured.

Her grandmother patted Kaya's shoulder. "You need to rest," she said. "Brown Deer is working near the tepees. Stay with her for a while. She'll want to hear about Speaking Rain, too."

Kaya found Brown Deer kneeling in the shade of a tepee, pounding dried salmon into fine pieces in a stone mortar. Kaya sat down next to her sister and hurriedly told her all about Speaking Rain.

"I have split feelings," Brown Deer admitted after Kaya had told her everything. "One feeling is happiness that our sister is alive and well. The other is sadness that she won't live with us."

"Aa-heh, I understand," Kaya said right away. "It's just the way I feel about your hope to marry Cut Cheek," she went on, surprised to hear herself confessing these feelings, too.

"But you like him, don't you?" Brown Deer asked, startled.

"I *do* like him," Kaya said. "And I know you love each other. I want you to marry. But at the same time, I don't want to lose you. So I'm happy and sad at the same time."

Brown Deer set down the stone pestle and put her hand on Kaya's arm. "We'll always be sisters, no matter what happens. You'll never lose me, I promise. Now we should think about how we can help Little Sister with her choice."

Kaya scrubbed at her eyes with the back of her hand. Brown Deer's kind words helped ease the ache in her chest. "I just wish there was some way for Speaking Rain to choose *both* Eetsa and White Braids!" she said.

Brown Deer scooped the ground-up salmon from the mortar and put it into a basket lined with dried fish skins. "We're friends with the Salish," she said. "We trade with them, and we join them to hunt buffalo. White Braids could live with us for a time. Is that what you mean?"

"White Braids doesn't speak our language—I don't think she'd want to leave her own people," Kaya admitted. Then she sat up straighter. She wasn't tired anymore—and she had an idea. "But Speaking Rain knows both languages now. Maybe she could go back and forth between White Braids and us."

"What do you mean?" Brown Deer asked. She stopped working and looked closely at Kaya.

"I mean, what if Speaking Rain chose to live part of the year with White Braids and part of the year with us?" Kaya said. "That way she could keep her vow to help White Braids, but she wouldn't have to give up our family completely."

Brown Deer's eyes lit up. "That's a new path to think about—a girl shared by two families and two tribes. We'll have to ask Kautsa for her counsel. But first I must finish this. Crane Song will be coming to check on me, and I still have so much work to do. Look, the sun is almost high overhead."

That evening Kaya and her parents tied up the canoe on the far shore and started walking upstream toward the Salish village. Eetsa carried a large woven bag filled with dried kouse roots to give to White Braids in thanks for saving her daughter. "I've told you how Speaking Rain came to be our child, haven't I," Eetsa said to Kaya.

Kaya hurried to keep up with Eetsa and Toe-ta. "We were both still babies, weren't we," she said. She'd heard this story many times.

Eetsa nodded. "You'd learned to walk," she said. "And Speaking Rain had just taken her first steps when her mother grew sick and died. Her mother was my dear, dear cousin. We'd grown up together, and when we both gave birth to daughters, we became closer still. When Speaking Rain lost her mother, and her father was gored to death on a buffalo hunt, Toe-ta and I took her to raise."

"But at first Speaking Rain didn't like you," Kaya added. "When you went to pick her up, she tried to squirm out of your arms!"

"She couldn't see me, but she knew from my touch that I wasn't her mother, so she fought me," Eetsa said. "When she hit me with her little fists, I thought, 'Tawts! She's a strong one! She'll be an independent girl.'"

"And you loved her anyway," Kaya said.

"I loved her *more* for that strong will of hers!" Eetsa corrected her.

"Now Kautsa's told us that Speaking Rain's made a

vow she won't break," Toe-ta said. "That's her strength showing itself."

"But she can't leave us!" Kaya insisted. "Maybe she can live with White Braids—and with us, too. Do you think she'd do that?"

"We've talked that over with Kautsa," Eetsa said with a frown. "But live with two families? That troubles me."

"We'll hear what Speaking Rain has to say," Toe-ta said firmly.

As they approached the Salish tepees, Kaya saw Speaking Rain standing near the path. Her head was tilted as if she could hear their footsteps approaching, and she was smiling. Kaya's heart lifted all over again to see her sister looking so healthy and well. "We're here!" Kaya called out.

Eetsa hurried to her daughter and hugged her tightly. "I feared for you!" she exclaimed. "And how I missed you! Now you're back again!"

Not saying a word, Toe-ta picked up Speaking Rain. She put her arms around his neck while he held her tightly against his chest for a long time. Then he set her gently down. White Braids, Two Hawks, and

Two Hawks's father waited a few paces away. With his hands Toe-ta thanked White Braids for saving his child's life, and he thanked Two Hawks and his father for bringing them together again.

"White Braids has prepared a meal for you," Two Hawks said. "Come to our tepee with us."

White Braids opened the tepee flaps to let in the cooling wind. As they sat there, shadows lengthened and the evening star began to rise. With Two Hawks interpreting, the talk was slow and respectful, and there was much to say. Kaya watched Speaking Rain's face as she turned first toward one speaker, then toward another, as if she were reaching out to them all.

Finally Toe-ta said gently, "Little Daughter, you haven't said much. What are your thoughts?"

Speaking Rain swallowed hard, and she sat up straighter. "Toe-ta, before you came here tonight, I told White Braids I'd made a vow always to help her, as she's helped me. 'We need each other now,' I said. She argued with me—she wants me to go back to you. But I can't break my vow. I owe her my life. You understand, don't you?" She turned to face White Braids and repeated what she'd said in Salish.

Right away White Braids spoke with her hands, *I love this girl very much, but I never wanted to take her from you! I only wanted her to live, to be well, to join her family again!*

I believe you, Eetsa signed to her. *But I also respect my daughter's vow and her need to keep it.*

Kaya could hold back no longer. Putting her hand on Speaking Rain's, she said, "Listen to me. I have an idea." Then she described how Speaking Rain could spend part of the year with White Braids and part with her own family. "If you do that, you can choose *both* of your mothers. Do you think that's possible, Little Sister?" As she spoke, Kaya heard her heart like a soft drumbeat, urging *Find a way, Find a way.*

"Do you mean go across the river with you for a few days, then come back here to join White Braids again?" Speaking Rain asked. "I could do that, but what would happen when the salmon fishing ends and we all leave the Big River?"

"Consider this," Toe-ta said. "You could go with us to Salmon River Country for the winter. Then, when it's digging time, we could take you back to the Palouse Prairie."

"You could meet White Braids there for the hard work of the digging season," Eetsa added.

Two Hawks spoke a moment with his father. "My father says some of my people can meet you at the Palouse Prairie, then bring you here to the Big River again."

"Everyone will help," Kaya said.

Finally Speaking Rain said slowly, "I can follow the path you've shown, Sister. I believe I can keep my vow but not hurt anyone. That's more than I ever hoped!"

"Then you'll come to us now?" Kaya asked her sister.

"Aa-heh," Speaking Rain said. "Katsee-yow-yow, Kaya."

When White Braids put her wrinkled hand on Speaking Rain's shoulder, Kaya knew she, too, was saying *Katsee-yow-yow*.

Kaya got to her feet. She was so light with relief that she felt like floating up to the small clouds racing toward the setting sun. "I'll carry your things, Sister. Let's go now while it's still light. The others want to welcome you back, too."

A few days later, Kaya was walking with
Speaking Rain to their tepees when she saw people
gathered on the plain upstream from the falls. The
fishermen caught only as many salmon as the women
were able to clean—when they'd caught their limit,
they got together for games, trading, and races. Now
Kaya saw a group of men sitting in two lines facing
each other, playing the Stick Game. They were
drumming to distract the ones trying to guess which
hands hid the small bone markers. They kept track
of the score with sticks stuck upright in the ground.
A few women stood behind the players, singing loudly
to add to the confusion. Jokes and shouts and songs
echoed across the valley.

"I hear so much commotion!" Speaking Rain said.
"They're playing the Stick Game, aren't they? Let's join
them."

"But some riders are getting ready to race their
horses," Kaya said. "Let's go there instead. I'll tell you
everything that's happening with the races!"

They hurried toward the long, flat stretch where

riders raced their horses. Kaya loved to watch the beautiful horses run, though it made her ache for Steps High. As she came closer, she realized that one of the riders on his spotted stallion was Cut Cheek. Brown Deer stood on the sidelines with some other young women. She had the twins with her.

"Is Cut Cheek going to race?" Kaya called as she and Speaking Rain came up to them.

"A band from the prairie challenged us!" Brown Deer said. Her eyes flashed with excitement. "They bet us that their best horse and rider could beat our best horse and rider. Our men chose Cut Cheek."

"I hear his stallion's fast!" Speaking Rain said.

"But look at that gray horse the other man is riding!" another girl said. "Those long legs, that sleek head! They say he's as swift as an antelope."

"But Cut Cheek's horse runs like a cougar!" Brown Deer said. "And Cut Cheek is a better rider, so he's sure to win. You'll see!"

The two men rode away from the others toward the far end of the race grounds.

"Cut Cheek's horse is straining at the bridle as if he can't wait to race!" Kaya told Speaking Rain. "The gray

horse is prancing and snorting. He's ready to run, too!"
Kaya held her breath as the starter raised his arm and
brought it down. "There they go!"

Both horses leaped forward like arrows shot from
bows. The riders lay low, their faces close to their
horses' necks. The horses lengthened out, running
faster with each stride, their tails streaming. Cut Cheek
and his horse seemed to blend into a single being,
running easily, as if they could race forever.

"Cut Cheek's ahead!" Kaya said. "He's pulling away
from the gray! They're coming to the finish line!"

"Cut Cheek wins!" Brown Deer cried out.

"I want to ride like he does!" Wing Feather cried.

"Nimíipuu won the bet!" Sparrow hopped around
like a jackrabbit.

As the riders rode back slowly, cooling their horses,
Brown Deer waited, smiling. Kaya knew her sister was
struggling not to let her feelings show, but her face
shone.

"You're proud of Cut Cheek, aren't you!" Kaya said.

"Aa-heh," Brown Deer said. "He rode well! But I
have something else to be happy about. Just before
I came to the race, Crane Song nodded at me!"

"Was her nod a good sign?" Kaya asked.

"It was only a little nod," Brown Deer admitted.

"But it must mean she's pleased with you," Speaking Rain assured her.

"At least a little pleased!" Brown Deer said. "I'm so glad! Would you two look after the twins for a while? I want to tell Cut Cheek—he'll be glad, too. I'll work even harder now!"

"Aa-heh, go tell him," Kaya said, giving Speaking Rain's hand a squeeze. "We'll take care of these bothersome little brothers of ours!"

As long as the run of salmon continued, Kaya helped Speaking Rain go back and forth across the river, staying a few days at a time with each of her two families. Now the season for fishing on the Big River was nearing an end. Speaking Rain would travel with Kaya and her family to higher country for berry picking and hunting, then down to Salmon River Country before snows came. But first there was work to be done while the men completed their fishing.

Kaya knelt beside Brown Deer under a tule mat

lean-to they'd made on the hillside above the river. Speaking Rain sat beside them, a box-turtle shell filled with green paint in her hands. Brown Deer had soaked a buffalo hide in the river and had staked it onto the ground in the shade. Now she was going to paint a design on the hide so that she could make it into a parfleche.

"Remember, we have to work quickly so the hide won't dry out. Paint bonds only to a damp hide," Brown Deer said. "I'll lay out the shapes and outline them. Kaya, you help me fill in the larger spaces with paint."

The tule mat shelter they'd made was a small one, but Tatlo managed to creep into its shade. Kaya scratched him behind his ears, and he went to sleep with his head on the edge of her dress.

Brown Deer had already covered the damp hide with a clear mixture of fish eggs to make it smooth and waterproof. Now she laid peeled willow sticks on it in a design of lines and triangles. She dipped a buffalo-bone tool into the paint, then expertly traced the design she'd made, drawing the edge of the bone tool down the hide in long, steady lines.

Kaya dipped in another tool, letting the porous bone soak up the lovely green paint made from river algae. Then she began spreading it where Brown Deer showed her.

"White Braids told me that soon she'll go back to her home country," Speaking Rain said. "I'll be sad to see her go."

"She's a fine woman to adopt you in this way, and you'll meet her again at the Palouse Prairie in the spring," Brown Deer said.

"Will Crane Song be coming with us for the berry picking, or will she go back to Cut Cheek's family when we leave?" Kaya asked her older sister.

Brown Deer's lips turned up a little as she drew. "Crane Song told me this morning that she'll be leaving us." She sat back and looked hard at the lines she'd made, then dipped her tool in the paint again. "She said I must work hard even when she's not around to keep an eye on me. But she told me she's satisfied I'll make Cut Cheek a good wife!" She sighed deeply, as if she'd been holding her breath for a long time.

"That's wonderful news!" Kaya exclaimed. "Why didn't you tell us?"

"I was afraid it might not be true," Brown Deer admitted.

"But it is!" Speaking Rain said. "I hear it in your voice. You're almost singing today."

"I feel like singing," Brown Deer said. "Cut Cheek said his parents will join us soon. They'll visit our family with their gifts. Then, in a little while, we'll visit them and give them ours. I'm making this parfleche for Cut Cheek's mother. I want it to be my very best work!"

"You've already made so many gifts," Kaya said. "Woven bags of beautifully dyed cords and grasses, and baskets filled with dried roots."

Brown Deer set aside her tool and picked up a little buckskin bag of powdered pigment. She took the container of green paint from Speaking Rain and gave her a large mussel shell in its place. "Hold this for me now," she said. "I want to mix up some red."

Speaking Rain held the mussel-shell bowl steady in her cupped hands as Brown Deer mixed the dry paint with water. "What will happen next?" she asked.

"First, Cut Cheek will live with us for a while," Brown Deer said. "Crane Song says he has to show my parents he'll be a good provider." She took two fresh bone tools from her kit and let them soak up the beautiful red paint, the color of sacred power.

"And when he proves himself?" Kaya asked.

"Then we'll make our home with my family for a time," Brown Deer said. "In hunting season, my parents will need our help more than Cut Cheek's family will. So I won't have to leave you now, after all." Her gaze caught Kaya's, and they both smiled.

"Soon you'll plan your marriage," Kaya said. The words were good ones.

Tatlo's paws twitched in his sleep—he was chasing rabbits in his dreams. Kaya stroked his warm head as she watched paint seep into the bone tools. She'd thought she would lose Brown Deer when she married, but that was not to be. She'd thought Speaking Rain would leave them forever, but that wasn't going to happen, either. If only she could get her horse back, her life would be complete. As she picked up her bone tool, she felt as if her full heart were glowing like the crimson paint.

Distant Fires

aya sat with Speaking Rain and some younger children on the dry, yellowed grass by the stream that wove its way across Weippe Prairie. For the first time in a long time, Kaya and her sister played with their dolls. At the end of summer, Nimíipuu women and girls worked hard to collect as much food as possible before cold weather came. Kaya couldn't work with the others because she was still mourning for her namesake, Swan Circling, and her sad feelings would spoil the roots and berries. Instead, she helped in other ways. Today she'd been busy carrying water, gathering wood for the fires, and sweeping around the tepees. Then, as the sun had grown hotter and hotter, she and Speaking Rain were given the job of looking after their little brothers and some other small children in the shade of the pines.

"Let's pretend we're setting up a camp," suggested Kaya, and the children nodded happily.

First Kaya made split-willow horses so that the little boys could play roundup. Then she made a fire ring of pebbles so that the little girls could pretend to cook with their miniature woven baskets. After that she set up a small tepee frame of willow branches and covered it with several old tule mats. The play tepee was big enough to hold several little girls, and they crawled inside with their dolls.

Kaya and Speaking Rain lay at the tepee entrance. As Kaya smoothed the delicate fringe on her doll's dress, she caught a glimpse of Brown Deer digging camas with the other women. It had been many snows since her hardworking older sister had played games like this one. Kaya knew that someday she would be too grown-up to play with her doll. And although she wanted to be strong, responsible, and a leader of her people, right now she was grateful to enjoy this game with the children.

After the salmon runs were over on the Big River, Kaya's band traveled here to the foothills of the mountains to dig roots, pick berries, and hunt.

Speaking Rain would spend part of the year with her
Salish mother, but until spring the sisters would be
together. Now Kaya's strongest fear was that she'd
never see her beloved horse again. Although Toe-ta told
her to choose another good mount of her own, she was
certain she could never love another horse as much as
she did Steps High.

As Kaya thought of her horse, she put a toy horse
made of a forked stick into Speaking Rain's hands.
"Will you hold this so I can hitch up the travois?"
Kaya asked. "Your doll can ride the horse when we've
got the travois loaded."

Speaking Rain held the stick horse steady between
the poles of the little travois, but instead of smiling
as the other children did, she frowned. "The smell of
smoke on the wind is growing stronger," she said.

"You've got a nose as keen as a bear's," Kaya teased.
She thought that because her sister was blind, her sense
of smell was especially sharp.

Speaking Rain lifted her chin and sniffed again.
"It smells like a grass fire," she said. "Is a new one
burning?"

Kaya shaded her eyes and gazed across the prairie.

To the west, the sun blazed above red clouds massed at the horizon. To the east, a thick haze hung low over the Bitterroot Mountains, which she had crossed with Two Hawks after they escaped from their enemies. When she drew a deep breath, smoke stung her nose, too. She licked her lips and tasted ash on her tongue. In this hot, dry season, lightning set many fires in the fields and forests, but she didn't see any new plumes of smoke in the surrounding hills. "Fires always flare up toward sundown when the wind rises," she said. "Are you troubled, Little Sister?"

"Aa-heh, I am troubled," Speaking Rain admitted. "Fire is like a mountain lion—you don't know when it might attack."

"I'd be troubled, too, if our scouts didn't always warn us of dangers," Kaya said.

"But our scouts are on the lookout for many things besides fires these days," Speaking Rain reminded her.

Kaya knew her sister was right. The scouts always kept watch for anything that might endanger the people, but now they were scouting out game trails and salt licks, too, as the best season for elk hunting approached. When Kaya thought of the elk hunts, she

felt a shiver of pride. Toe-ta was one of the most
experienced hunters, and the men had asked him to
serve as headman for the hunts. Toe-ta's wyakin, a
wolf, had given him strong hunting power, and the
hunters needed to kill many elk to feed everyone
through the long, cold season to come. The elk hunts
would also be a chance for Cut Cheek to prove his
worth as a provider so that he and Brown Deer would
be allowed to marry.

Speaking Rain cocked her head. "I hear horses
coming this way," she said.

Kaya heard the hoofbeats, too, and got to her
feet. "They're coming slowly," she said. "The
horses would be galloping if scouts were bringing
a warning."

Soon Kaya could see a line of men riding out of
the woods on the far side of the prairie. They were
followed by women and children on horseback, pack
horses, and other women whose mounts pulled
loaded travois. Their dogs trotted alongside the horses,
wagging their tails as the camp dogs rushed out to
meet them.

"It's the hunting party that went over the Buffalo

Trail last year to hunt," Kaya said. "Come on, let's welcome them back!"

The children didn't need urging—they were already hurrying to meet the buffalo hunters and the women who'd gone along with them to run the camp and prepare the meat. Kaya grabbed Speaking Rain's hand and they ran to greet them, too.

After everyone had greeted the hunters, and the dried meat and hides had been distributed, the young men took their horses to the stream. When the horses had drunk their fill, the men splashed them with the cool water, then let them dry themselves by rolling in the grass. Kaya and Speaking Rain eagerly joined their young uncles, who always brought news and stories. Tatlo, growing big and long-legged now, left the milling dog pack and pressed himself against Kaya's legs.

Jumps Back tugged Kaya's braid to tease her. He was a short, easygoing fellow with a big grin. After Brown Deer turned him down in the courtship dance and chose Cut Cheek instead, Jumps Back had said he hoped she was happy with her choice. Kaya liked him for that generous thought. "We've been gone so long, you girls are almost grown-up!" Jumps Back said. "I bet the boys serenade you with their flutes!"

"Not me!" Speaking Rain said with a giggle.

"Not me!" Kaya echoed her sister.

"Do your cousins still call you that silly nickname, Magpie?" Jumps Back asked, nudging Kaya's arm with his and laughing.

Kaya laughed, too. "Nobody calls me Magpie anymore—except once in a while," she said. But to change the subject, she pointed to a young stallion getting to his feet, bits of grass stuck in his black mane and tail. "I haven't seen that bay before. He looks fast."

"Aa-heh, he is fast," Jumps Back said. "I chased him hard on my best horse to get a rope on him. Four sleeps ago we came upon a few horses led by a rogue stallion. He drove off his herd before we could get close, but this young stallion hung back from the others, and I gave chase. He'd been driven off by the older horse, I think."

"I didn't know there was a herd of untamed horses in this area," Kaya said.

"Some seem tame," Jumps Back said. "We think they're Nimíipuu horses. We're going to try to find them again before the snows come."

Kaya's pulse sped. "Nimíipuu horses!" she exclaimed. "The ones stolen from us last year? Was my horse one of them? Steps High has a star on her forehead, remember?" Hearing the excitement in her voice, Tatlo gazed up at her, his tail thumping against her leg.

Jumps Back rubbed his forehead as he thought hard. "I'm not sure," he said. "There were a few spotted horses in the herd, but I didn't get a good look."

"I guess I'm hoping for too much," Kaya said with disappointment. "I last saw my horse in Salish country. She couldn't be back in these mountains."

"Don't be too sure about that," Jumps Back said kindly. "A stolen horse can stray off if it isn't tied to another horse while it gets accustomed to the herd. Your horse could have strayed and headed back this way, maybe searching for you. If we can track down those horses again, we'll find out."

But Kaya was almost afraid to hope—it would hurt so badly to have her hopes dashed. Instead, she asked Many Deer, one of her uncles, "Did you make any good trades in your travels?"

"We met up with some hunters from the north,"

Many Deer said. He was known as a good hunter but was even better known for his short temper. "They wanted to trade for our best horses, but we refused. Instead, we traded a pack horse for three buffalo calfskin robes and some rawhide rope. That was a good trade!" His broad face flushed as he boasted. "And I got something they say came from the east, maybe from men with pale, hairy faces. Look here!" He opened his pack and took out a red-and-white bead, holding it out for Kaya to examine.

"It's pretty," Kaya said hesitantly—she remembered her grandmother's warnings about dangers from pale-faced men.

Speaking Rain was stroking Tatlo. Kaya took her sister's hand and guided her fingertip to the bead. "It's smooth!" Speaking Rain exclaimed. "Maybe Brown Deer could sew it on a gift she's making for the wedding exchange."

Kaya leaned forward to take a better look at the pretty bead. "Would you trade it to me for a basket of dried salmon eggs?" she asked Many Deer.

At that moment Tatlo thrust his muzzle into Many Deer's pack, seized a small bundle in his sharp teeth, and shook it. Many Deer aimed a kick at Tatlo and caught the dog in the chest, sending him tumbling. "Stay out!" he hissed.

"My dog!" Kaya cried.

But Tatlo wasn't hurt. He lunged to his feet and placed himself between Kaya and Many Deer, baring his teeth and growling, ready to protect her at any cost.

Many Deer stepped back and put away the bead. "Forget it! Magpies have a lot to learn about making a trade!" he said scornfully.

"Aa-heh, you're right," Kaya said quickly. She held Tatlo firmly by the scruff of his neck and tried to think what Swan Circling would have done in a situation like this one. "I'm sorry my dog got into your pack," Kaya said after a moment. "Don't let that spoil your homecoming."

Jumps Back tapped Many Deer on the shoulder. "Come on," he said to the bad-tempered fellow. "We're tired and hungry. The boys will look after our horses while we eat." As they walked away, Jumps Back glanced at Kaya with a look of approval that said she'd handled the tense moment well.

Kaya took a deep breath to settle herself. More and

more lately she'd been thinking about Swan Circling.
Kaya realized that her thoughts were now lighter
when she remembered her hero. Perhaps sad feelings
would no longer spoil the food that Kaya gathered.
She wanted to talk over her thoughts with her grandmother.

Toward sundown, Kaya found her grandmother
and Brown Deer cutting tule reeds in a marshy place
at the edge of the prairie. They bent low to cut off the
tall reeds. "Here you are, Granddaughter," Kautsa
greeted her. "Come bundle up these tules so we can
take them to the village to dry."

Kaya carried an armload of tules to a sandy spot
and wrapped cord around them. "Kautsa, I've been
thinking," she said.

"Have you been thinking how to make your dog
behave better?" Kautsa asked with a smile. "I saw
Many Deer kick Tatlo when he got into the pack."

Was there anything her sharp-eyed grandmother
didn't see? Kaya said, "I was angry about that kick,
but I apologized for Tatlo."

"Tawts!" Kautsa said. "You must treat everyone well if you want to be a leader like your namesake someday. It's easy to be kind to a pleasant person, but it takes strength to be kind to an angry one. Now tell me what else you've been thinking." As she spoke she cut more tules, passing them to Kaya.

"I've been thinking a lot about my namesake," Kaya said, careful not to say the name of the dead out loud. "I've mourned her death for many moons, and I think my heart feels lighter now."

"Are you sure?" Kautsa asked.

"I'm sure," Kaya said.

Kautsa stood up, put her hand on Kaya's shoulder, and looked into her eyes. "If the time of mourning has passed in your heart, will you join us to pick berries?"

"Aa-heh," Kaya said firmly. "My namesake was always a strong worker. I want to live up to her name."

"Tawts! Let's take these tules back to the village," Kautsa said. "We need to fix our evening meal."

Brown Deer straightened and slipped her knife into the workbag on her belt.

"We need your help with the berries, Sister," she said as they picked up the bundles of tules. "Brings

Word told us this will be the last time she leads us in the berry picking. She's getting too old and her eyesight is failing. She feels it's time to find someone to take her place. Who do you think would be a good leader?"

Kaya knew that for quite some time the women had been talking about who would replace Brings Word. She'd been thinking about it herself. "I think our mother would be a good leader," she said without hesitation. "Eetsa is very considerate of others, and she's a good judge of where berries are thickest and when they're ready to be picked. She always leaves some on the bushes so there'll be more the next season. But shouldn't the next leader be one of our chief's own daughters?"

"Not necessarily," Kautsa said. Though she carried a heavy load, she walked with vigorous strides. "To Soar Like An Eagle isn't the son of the old chief, but he's the wisest and the bravest among our men. That's why the council selected him to lead us."

"He showed his courage when he was very young, didn't he?" Kaya asked. She loved to hear stories about warriors and their deeds.

"Aa-heh," Kautsa agreed. "As a young man he was

hunting buffalo when a prairie fire swept across the plains toward the hunting camp. The horses bolted and ran away. There seemed to be no escape from the rushing flames—the men were sure to be killed! But To Soar Like An Eagle quickly set a fire of his own and burned a patch of the dry grass. Then he and the others lay down on the hot ashes as the prairie fire passed around the burned-off place. He saved many lives that day!"

Kaya frowned in concentration. She tried to imagine standing her ground in front of a wall of flame in order to set a backfire—would she ever be able to think so fast and act with such courage? "To Soar Like An Eagle is very brave," she said.

"Aa-heh, he is brave, but above all else, he's just and he's generous," Kautsa added. She slid the bundle of tules off her shoulders and placed it near the doorway of their tepee. "Wait here a moment, Granddaughter," she said as she ducked inside.

Brown Deer and Kaya put down their bundles, too. In a moment Kautsa appeared again, the hat she'd woven last winter for Kaya in her hand. Kaya had planned to wear the new hat this past spring when she dug roots for her First Foods Feast, but because she was in mourning, she hadn't been able to dig with the other girls and women. Kautsa had kept the hat with her own things.

"Soon we'll start berry picking, and after that we'll go with the hunters on the elk hunt," Kautsa said. "You'll need much strength in the days ahead if you're to work as your namesake did to feed the people. Now it's time for you to wear this." She placed the hat firmly on Kaya's head.

"Katsee-yow-yow," Kaya said softly, touching the single feather that decorated the top. She was eager to join the others again. And when they went with the hunters farther into the mountains, she might find her horse again, too. She narrowed her eyes as the evening wind carried more ash from distant fires. "I'm ready, Kautsa," she said.

The Rogue Stallion's Herd

The days were growing shorter now. Kaya heard owls screeching at night and saw geese flying high—signs that the coming winter would be a hard one. But berries were especially thick and plump this year, and with Brings Word's leadership, the women and girls were able to pick and store a great many.

As the berry season came to an end, the band split up. Many journeyed down to Salmon River Country to set up their winter village in the sheltered valley there. Kaya traveled with her family and the hunting party higher into the mountains for the elk hunts. The men rode ahead, leading the way, the women and children following with travois and pack horses. Raven, Fox Tail, and other young boys brought up the rear, driving extra horses to carry back the meat.

As they ascended the trail, Kaya looked out across steep, rocky hillsides split by stony gulches. Whirring ladybugs swarmed around the horses. The mountainsides glowed with deep green heather and red-orange huckleberry bushes. All around, a blue haze of smoke rose from the valleys and tinted the sky gray with ash. Though cold weather was not far off, the days were dry with no sign of rain—it was still the season of fires. The scouts constantly scanned the mountains and skies for signs of danger.

As the women set up the hunting camp, Kaya helped raise the tepees, then took the twins to where Kautsa and Brown Deer were preparing a meal. The boys were hungry, so Brown Deer gave them some pine nuts to nibble on while the deer meat cooked.

"Speaking Rain was glad to go down to Salmon River Country," Brown Deer said to Kaya.

"Aa-heh," Kaya agreed. "The fires in these mountains trouble her."

"I'm not afraid of fire," Sparrow boasted. "It can't hurt me!"

"Speaking Rain knows better—fire *can* hurt you," Brown Deer corrected him. She placed heated stones into the water in the cooking basket, stirring them so that they wouldn't scorch the basket.

"You must always respect the power of fire, Grandson," Kautsa added sternly as she put deer meat into the boiling water. "Fire is a great gift, but it has its dangers, too. You remember the story of the boy who brought fire down from the heavens, don't you?"

"Tell it again!" the twins begged.

Kaya smiled at her little brothers—and at her grandmother. She thought Kautsa liked to tell stories almost as much as children liked to hear them. And although winter was the proper season for storytelling, Kautsa couldn't resist telling one now.

Kautsa sat down on a tule mat and gave her full attention to the story. "Long ago, Nimíipuu had no fire," she began. "They could see fire in the sky, but it belonged to Hun-ya-wat, who kept it in great black bags. When the cloud bags bumped together, they crashed and thundered, and fire flashed through the hole that was made."

"That fire was lightning!" Wing Feather knew this story well.

"Aa-heh, it was lightning," Kautsa went on. "How

the people longed to get that fire! Without it they couldn't cook their food or keep themselves warm. The medicine men beat their drums, trying to get the fire down from the sky, but no fire came.

"Then a young boy said he knew how to get the fire. Everyone laughed at him, and the medicine men said, 'How can a mere boy do what we aren't able to do?' But the boy waited patiently. When he saw black clouds on the horizon, he bathed himself and scrubbed himself clean with fir branches to prepare for his task. Then he wrapped an arrowhead inside a piece of cedar bark and put it with his bow and arrow. He placed the white shell he wore around his neck on the ground, and asked his wyakin to help him shoot his arrow into the black cloud that held fire.

"The medicine men thought they should kill the boy so he wouldn't anger Hun-ya-wat. But the people said, 'Let him try to capture the fire. If he fails, we can kill him then.' The boy wasn't afraid. He waited until a thundercloud loomed overhead, rumbling and crashing as it came. Then he raised his bow and shot his arrow straight upward. Suddenly, everyone heard a tremendous crash and saw a flash of fire in the sky.

The burning arrow, like a falling star, came hurtling down among them. It struck the boy's white shell, resting on the ground, and set it aflame.

"Shouting with joy, the people rushed forward to get the fire. They lighted sticks and dry bark and hurried to their tepees to start fires of their own. Children and old people, too, laughed and sang.

"When the excitement had died down, people asked about the boy. But he was nowhere to be seen. There lay his shell, burned so that it showed the colors of fire. Near it lay his bow. Men tried to shoot with that bow, but not even the strongest man could bend it.

"The boy was never seen again. But," and here Kautsa touched the beautiful shells that fastened her braids, "his abalone shell is still touched with the colors of flame. And the fire he brought down from the clouds burns in the center of every tepee," she said, finishing the story. Then she fixed her steady gaze on the twins, and the sharp lines between her eyes deepened. "Listen to me. You two must try to be as strong and generous as that boy of long ago."

Kaya was glad to hear the old story another time, but she thought again of Speaking Rain's worry about fires. She vowed to keep a sharp watch for them as she searched the surrounding countryside for signs of her horse.

On the day before the hunt, Toe-ta hobbled the lead mare with a rope attached to her forelegs so that she couldn't wander away—he wanted the horses close by so that they could be easily rounded up before first light. He invited the hunters into his tepee to talk over plans for the hunt. Then the men gathered in the sweat lodge to make themselves clean. They thanked Hun-ya-wat for all His gifts and prayed that they would be worthy of the animals they needed for food. Kaya could hear their prayer songs rising up to the Creator.

That night everyone slept only a short while. Kaya heard Toe-ta and Cut Cheek rising in the dark to join the other men. They took their bows and arrows and put on headdresses of animal hides to disguise their human scent. Kaya, Eetsa, and Brown Deer quickly dressed themselves. They rode away from the camp long before sunrise while the elk were still out feeding or returning to their bedding place from the salt lick.

Everyone dismounted near the valley where scouts had discovered the elk herd. Raven and the boys looked after the horses while the others went forward on foot. Quickly and quietly, the hunters took up positions at the narrow end of the valley, downwind from the elk. At the wide end of the valley, the women and girls fanned out in a broad V to drive the elk ahead of them toward the waiting hunters. They took care not to startle the elk as they moved slowly forward. If the elk started running, they'd plunge right past the hidden men, who wouldn't be able to get clear shots.

Kaya concentrated on the rustle of the elk moving through the plumed beargrass. She could make out the tips of their antlers, the flash of tan rumps, and the flickers of ear tips. Even in the faint light she could see their tracks on the worn game trails. Birds flew up all around her, and from time to time a woman added her whistle to the birdcalls, making her position known to the others.

Then Kaya remembered that she should be on the lookout for fires, too. She scanned the mountain slope at the far end of the valley. There was no sign of smoke on the plateau there, but shapes moved among the pines, and she thought she heard a distant whinny. Holding her breath, she stood still and peered through the dim light. Gradually she made out horses emerging from the trees to graze. Kaya's heart sped. Could that be the small herd that the buffalo hunters had seen? Could Steps High be with them? Kaya stared hard, but the horses were too far off for her to see them clearly.

Kaya walked slowly forward again, but her racing thoughts tumbled ahead, one over the other. What if she slipped away from the others to get a better look at the horses? Couldn't she run up to the ridge for a better view and be back before the slow-moving elk herd reached the hunters? Or couldn't she get a mount and ride close enough to the horses to whistle for Steps High if she was with them? Maybe she could round up the horses by herself—think how proud of her every-one would be!

Then, right in front of her, a pair of magpies flew out of their dome-shaped nest in a thorny bush. Crying boldly, they swooped upward among the other birds. Like an uplifted hand, the sight of the magpies halted Kaya's racing thoughts. No, she must not act in such

a way that she could be called Magpie ever again! It
would be irresponsible to go after the horses by herself.
She must follow in Swan Circling's footsteps and do
only what was best for her people. She must work
with the others so that there would be food for all.
Whistling to signal her place in the group, she drove
the elk forward to the waiting hunters.

The hunters' arrows were swift and their aim was
true. Many elk gave themselves to Nimíipuu that
morning. Then the women and girls prepared the meat
to be packed back to the camp, where they would cook
some of it and dry the rest. Kaya could tell by Brown
Deer's shining eyes that Cut Cheek had hunted well.
He'd given the elk he'd killed to her parents as a sign
of respect.

Kaya couldn't wait any longer to talk to her father
about the horse herd she'd seen at sunup. She found
Toe-ta lifting a heavy bundle of meat onto a travois and
described the horses she'd seen. "Jumps Back thinks
they're our horses, Toe-ta. Steps High might be with
them," she added, trying to hold down her excitement.

Toe-ta put his firm hand on her shoulder. "Daughter, there's not much chance that your horse could be with that herd."

"But there is some chance, isn't there?" Kaya insisted. "Steps High could have strayed off and come back this way."

Toe-ta thought for a long moment. "That's possible. We'll go look for the herd," he said. "I'll ask Raven to come along—he's not needed here right now. Let's see what we can find."

Kaya mounted a chestnut horse and rode out of the valley behind Raven and Toe-ta. They followed a game trail that led upward toward the plateau where she'd seen horses grazing. The sun was high overhead, and heat waves shimmered over the stony hillside. She was sure she'd seen the horses near those pines ahead, but now there was no sign of them. Had the lead mare taken the herd where it was cooler?

The trail left by the horses curved around the mountain and angled down the northern side. Kaya's gaze swept across slopes dotted with stunted firs and hunchbacked pines, bent down by past winter snows. Deep gulches jagged down the mountain in every direction. The herd could be in any one of them. Would they be able to find the horses before they had to rejoin the hunting party, now a long way away?

The trail descended more and more steeply, and after a time they found themselves in a narrow canyon where a thick grove of tall firs grew. Spears of sunlight shafted down through the canopy of branches, and the shadowed air was a little cooler here. A small stream snaked through the trees. Toe-ta signaled Kaya and Raven to halt their horses and let them drink.

Kaya slipped off the chestnut horse she rode and knelt upstream from the horses, drinking from her cupped hands. The spring water was clean and cold, and she was very grateful for it. When she glanced up again, she realized that the patches of dappled light in the grove of trees were moving. Slowly and silently, as if in a dream, a few horses appeared in the grove— and then a few more. Coming to the watering place, they stepped around fallen logs. When the lead mare spotted intruders, she halted in her tracks, and the other horses came to a stop behind her.

Kaya got slowly to her feet. Toe-ta and Raven stood, too. Then Toe-ta pointed to a horse barely visible behind the others, a horse whose black forehead was marked with a white star.

"Steps High!" Kaya whispered, almost afraid to breathe. In the same moment that she recognized her beloved horse, a long-legged, spotted foal crowded against Steps High's side—her horse had a little one!

Toe-ta climbed onto his stallion Runner again. Raven jumped back onto his own horse, too. "Whistle for your horse, Daughter," Toe-ta said softly. "She'll recognize your whistle. Call her to you."

Kaya's heart thudded, and her lips were dry. She licked them and managed to make the shrill whistle with which she'd called Steps High so many times. Her horse's ears shot up. Kaya whistled again, and Steps High began to move toward her, the foal following closely. "Come on, girl," Kaya urged her horse. She whistled a third time—just as the air was split by a stallion's scream of fury. The rogue stallion had come down from the hill to claim his herd and protect it.

The rogue was a reddish bay with a black mane and tail. Swift as an antelope, he plunged through the trees and across the clearing to guard his mares. His nostrils flared and his eyes shone with defiance as he screamed his challenge at the intruders. Then he lowered his head almost to the ground, his neck out-stretched as he dove at the mares, driving them into a bunch.

Toe-ta had his rawhide rope ready. Raven coiled his rope, too, and began to circle around the milling horses. "Whistle again!" Raven cried to Kaya. "Keep calling your horse! She wants to come to you!"

Kaya repeated her whistle. Steps High swung around, trying to elude the rogue, but each time she swerved away from him, he drove her back with the other horses.

Now Toe-ta on Runner circled the herd in the other direction to distract the rogue. The rogue pawed the ground, snorting and trumpeting to drive off the challenger, screaming fiercely that these mares belonged to him alone!

When the rogue's back was to her, Kaya rode around behind the herd. Steps High made another dash for her, breaking away from the other horses. Kaya swung her rope and swiftly threw it over Steps High's head—she had her horse again! In a burst of

speed, Kaya on the chestnut horse rode away from
the herd. Leading Steps High, the foal running right
behind, they galloped off.

Raven on his horse quickly caught up to Kaya.
"Let's race!" he called to her with a grin. "Is your
horse still fast?"

Toe-ta came galloping after, and they rode up the
valley, the rogue's shrill trumpeting echoing behind
them.

Stones clattered from under the horses' hooves as
they ascended the narrow trail that led over the ridge.
Heading back to the hunting party, they made their
way through broad canyons and deep gulches. As they
rode, Toe-ta studied the sky and the puffy, misshapen
white clouds that rose on the updrafts. He seemed
worried. In a narrow canyon, he said, "Wait here. I
want to get a look at the countryside from the crest of
that hill."

Kaya slipped from the chestnut horse and went
to Steps High. Her horse shuddered, then pushed
her head affectionately against Kaya's shoulder. Kaya
ran her palm down the muzzle, soft as doeskin, and
stroked the powerful jaw and sleek neck. She gazed

into Steps High's dark, glistening eyes and felt her own fill with tears. "You've chosen to be my horse again," she whispered. "Katsee-yow-yow, my beautiful one!"

The foal nuzzled Steps High's flank. "Raven, look at her foal!" Kaya cried. She smiled at the foal's short brush of a tail, long legs, and big eyes. "Isn't he handsome with all the black spots? Won't he be—"

The sound of a running horse interrupted her excited words. Toe-ta reined in Runner, hooves plowing the sand, and motioned for Kaya to mount the chestnut horse again. "There's a fire just over that ridge. The wind is spreading it this way. We have to get out of this gulch." He kept his voice low, but she heard the warning in his tone.

Kaya glanced at the ridgeline. She saw a plume of smoke, but it was thin and white—it didn't look threatening. Three or four small spot fires burned near the top of the ridge, but the grass there was thin and sparse and the blazes no larger than cooking fires. What had Toe-ta seen that alarmed him so?

"Stay with me and keep close," Toe-ta said. He urged Runner ahead on the narrow game trail that ran down the gulch. Kaya jumped back on the

chestnut, clasped Steps High's rope tightly, and
followed her father, with Raven coming right behind.
When she looked back again only moments later,
more fires burned from sparks blown into the brush.
And now she could hear something hissing and growling in the distance—like a mountain lion, the fire was
leaping after them!

Trapped by Fire!

❈ CHAPTER 12 ❈

The twisted gulch they rode down was narrow and steep-sided. Kaya rode as fast and as close to Toe-ta as she could, keeping Steps High right behind her. The foal ran, too, his head at his mother's flank. Across the gulch, small fires flapped along the ridge where two winds met, pushing the fire back and forth between them. That side, the north one, was thickly wooded with juniper and fir trees. Kaya knew fire would burn fiercely in the dense trees. The south side, where they rode, was covered with bunchgrass and a few pines scattered here and there. Fire would burn more lightly on this side, though in the baking sun, the air itself felt like fire. Her eyes stung, and her throat burned with every breath.

In a gust of wind, the wavering fire across from

them dipped down into the pines. Swiftly, it grew and grew. Kaya watched in alarm as burning pinecones began to swirl through the air, starting spot fires farther down the slope. The smoke blackened and boiled upward. Fire began to growl like a bear as it spread both up and down the slope. Could it keep pace with them as they galloped their horses down the gulch toward the open end and safety on the plain beyond? The frantic horses couldn't be held back— every fiber of their beings wanted escape.

Other creatures also sought escape from the windswept fire. Frightened deer, their brown eyes wide, leaped out of the thickets and bounded to the south side of the gulch, racing up toward the ridge. Jackrabbits came, too, and ground squirrels. Clouds of grasshoppers whirred up out of the smoke. Patches of brush under the trees burst into flame, flushing grouse and quail. When Kaya looked back, she saw Raven lying low on his horse, one hand cupped over his nose and mouth. Kaya thought only, *Stay with Toe-ta! Take care of Steps High and her foal!*

Fearfully, she looked across the gulch again. Heat waves heaved and buckled above the spreading fire.

Fiery pine needles rose up like sparks flying. Burning twigs snapped and cracked. Juniper trees began exploding in the intense heat. But the open end of the gulch wasn't far off now—was it? Kaya coughed and her eyes teared in the bitter smoke. It was almost too hot now to breathe, and fear was another fire in her chest. It was all she could do to cling to her horse as it bolted behind Toe-ta's along the narrow mountain-goat trail.

Then, with a roar, the ground fire on the north slope suddenly exploded into the treetops. Kaya saw the topmost branches become a crimson tent of flames. The trees burned from the tops down, like torches. A high wind gusted up from the burning trees, making the boiling fires hotter still. Wind snapped off branches with a sound like bones cracking. It lifted logs into the air. The fire swirl spun down to the bottom of the gulch and burst across onto the south slope below them. With a stab of pure terror, Kaya realized that now it burned ahead of them, too, blankets of black smoke covering their escape route. The panicked horses doubled back, bumping into each other, rearing and snorting in terror.

Kaya fought to stay on her plunging horse. Steps

High reared again and again—would she fall backward on the slipping stones? Would the foal be trampled? Terrified, Kaya thought, *Have I found my horse only to lose her to fire?*

Toe-ta scanned the steep-sided gulch, looking for a possible escape route over the ridge above them, but rimrock created a barrier just below the top. Could they find a way through the barrier? Kaya saw there was no choice—they had to try.

"Stay with me!" Toe-ta shouted over the howling roar. "Don't fall back!" His face was black with smoke and fierce with determination. Did he see a way out of this fiery trap? He gestured for Kaya and Raven to follow as he turned Runner toward the steep slope above them and urged him upward. Raven's horse clambered up behind, its powerful haunches knotted with effort. Kaya forced the chestnut to follow and yanked on Steps High's rope to bring her along. The foal sprang over the rocks like a deer. But could the horses climb faster than the fire? Racing for their lives, they struggled upward.

Ashes, like flakes of snow, swirled across Kaya's sight. Burning embers fell onto her head and shoulders,

stinging her hands when she brushed them away. On
the loose stones, the horses' hooves slipped backward
with each lunge until they gained a broad shelf not far
below the rimrock barrier. Then the wind suddenly
split the smoke, and for a moment Kaya saw the barrier
clearly. Was that slash a crevice, a way through? Could
they reach it? Again Toe-ta signaled for them to follow.
Raven urged his horse after Toe-ta as the curtain of
smoke swung closed behind them.

Before Kaya could follow, Steps High began to rear,
whipping her head back and forth frantically. Kaya
looked back—the foal wasn't there! Was it lost in the
smoke, caught by the rushing fire? Frantic to find her
foal, Steps High thrashed her head, tearing the rawhide
rope from Kaya's grip. "Stop!" Kaya screamed. "Don't
go back!" But, searching for her foal, Steps High had
already plunged down the slope and vanished into the
smoke.

Kaya tried to rein in the chestnut, turn it back after
Steps High, but the panicked horse resisted. Without
thinking twice, Kaya slipped off the chestnut, which
pushed on up the slope where Toe-ta and Raven had
disappeared. Kaya whirled around. Smoke surrounded

her on all sides. Through the smoke, the sun was blood red. She stood alone. Her eyes felt blistered by the heat, and she cupped her hands over them. *I must be strong!* she thought. *I must not give up!*

When Kaya opened her eyes, Steps High was lunging out of the blackness, her foal again at her side. She'd reclaimed her young one! As Steps High came near, Kaya leaped to catch the rawhide rope still encircling her neck. With her horse pulling her, Kaya stumbled alongside as they started uphill again. Jagged stones tore at her feet. Her ankle twisted and she lost her footing. She fell uphill onto her stomach beneath her horse's legs. Kaya rolled onto her side. Would the hooves crush her? But Steps High curled her forelegs and managed to bring her sharp hooves down beyond Kaya's head. "Katsee-yow-yow!" Kaya cried. But she knew that on foot she couldn't keep up with her horse. Steps High would have to let Kaya ride if they were both to escape the fire.

When Steps High turned uphill again, Kaya saw her one chance to mount—if her horse threw her off, there would be no second try. Using all her remaining strength, Kaya scrambled onto a boulder, clasped Steps

High's mane with both hands, and dragged herself onto her horse's back. Steps High shuddered but accepted Kaya's weight—her horse hadn't forgotten! Kaya rejoiced to be one again with Steps High. But which way should they go? She had no idea. The blowing smoke created a vast black cave with no opening. She'd seen a crevice in the barrier, but where was it? There? Or there? Which way might offer escape? If they went the wrong way, the fire would seize them!

Then Kaya heard a shrill whistle, one high, wavering note that cut through the roar. Could it be green wood singing in the flames? The whistle came again, more urgently. *Here! Here!* the whistle sang. It came to her that Toe-ta was whistling to her, signaling the way. She looked toward the sound but could see nothing. Then a gust of wind knifed through the smoke, and again she spotted the crevice, with a deep game trail leading toward it.

Kaya turned Steps High along the game trail toward the opening. With the foal pressing after, they gained the base of the barrier. Now Kaya felt wind pouring through the opening. Steps High felt the wind, too, and nosed forward, though she balked at the

narrow passage. "Go!" Kaya urged her horse. Steps
High moved one step, then another. Kaya's knees
scraped the sides as they slipped through, the foal
following. On the far side Kaya saw the ridgeline right
above them. She clasped Steps High even more tightly
with her knees and pressed her face into the black
mane. "A little farther—we're almost there!" she cried.
A few more steps and they had reached the crest.

Still panicked, Steps High started to tear down
the other side, stones showering out from under her
hooves. Toe-ta on lathered Runner was riding hard
back up the hill, looking for Kaya just as Steps High
had searched for her foal. He swerved Runner, grasped
the rope around Steps High's neck, and brought her to
a standstill before she could injure herself and Kaya.
Steps High's chest heaved, and her coat was drenched
with lather. The foal's legs shook with fatigue. Kaya
slumped forward. Her breath rasped in her throat and
her lungs ached from the smoke.

Toe-ta threw his arm around her shoulders. "Rest a
moment!" he said. "We're safe here."

Kaya gazed around. The fire didn't threaten them
here because an earlier one had already burned off the

hillside. Ash-gray patches of sage still smoldered. Juni-per stumps smoked. In some places fire had swept by so quickly that it had left the brush only singed. Farther down the stony hillside, Raven on his horse made his way to the narrow river below, where deer and elk stood chest-high in the water. He glanced back and raised his hand to her—they'd made it to safety!

"You fell behind," Toe-ta said in his deep voice. "I thought I'd lost you."

"Steps High ran away from me to find her foal," Kaya gasped. "When I caught her again, I lost my way. But you whistled to me! I followed your whistle and found the opening. Katsee-yow-yow, Toe-ta." Her voice shook, and she thought she was laughing until she felt tears running down her cheeks.

Toe-ta wiped away her tears with his palm. "I'm so proud of your courage, Daughter," he said. "You saved yourself, and your horse, too. But what was that whistle you heard?"

"Your whistle," Kaya repeated.

Gazing into her eyes, Toe-ta slowly shook his head. "I was headed for the river when I realized you weren't behind me. Right away, I started back after you. But I didn't whistle to you. That must have been the Stick People. They showed you the way."

"The Stick People?" Kaya said.

"Aa-heh," Toe-ta said. "I think they saw you needed help, and they gave it."

Kaya's head was spinning, but she remembered she must leave a gift for the Stick People. "What can I give them?" she asked Toe-ta.

"We'll leave them many gifts," Toe-ta said. "Now let's get to the river. The horses need water, and we do, too." Still clasping Steps High's rope, he began to lead Kaya on her horse down the burned-over hillside, puffs of ashes rising at their feet.

Gifts

s the hunting party rode out of the mountains to join the rest of the band in Salmon River Country, the skies turned gray with heavy clouds. Soon the first autumn rains began to fall. After the long, dry season of fires, the rain was a blessing. Kaya pulled her deerskin robe over her head, but she lifted her face to the rain. It would soon turn to snow, but now it bathed her cheeks and forehead with a soft, light touch. The rain dripped from the branches she rode under, raising sweet scents of pine and fir. Drops of it beaded in Steps High's mane and on her foal's eyelashes. Kaya stroked her horse's warm, wet neck and smiled to see the foal, which she'd named Sparks Flying, splashing through the shallow stream.

Even in the rain, the woods around Kaya were filled with color. She saw aspen trunks washed to pure white

and the larch needles shining yellow. Ferns had dried
to a dark orange, rosebushes were red-leafed, and gilded
mosses hung from the fir boughs. A snake slithered
across the trail with a green gleam. Blackbirds flocked
together for their flight south. Red-sided trout leaped
from the stream after insects, and on the opposite shore
Kaya saw a brown bear gorging itself on fish.

Now deer and elk were coming down to lower
country to forage. As she rode across a clearing, Kaya
saw a bull elk running through the brush. He lifted
his legs high and tilted back his head so that his huge
antlers could slip through the branches as he raced like
a scout bringing a message. Kaya's heart swelled. She
felt how strongly she loved her beautiful homeland and
all the creatures that shared it with Nimíipuu.

When the hunting party reached the wintering
place, Tatlo burst from the village dog pack and came
running to meet Kaya. Bounding alongside Steps High,
he barked repeatedly as if to say, *You're back, you're back!*
And when Kaya dismounted, he licked her cheek over
and over again with his warm, rough tongue.

Kaya turned out Steps High and Sparks Flying
with the other horses. Then, with Tatlo at her side, she

ran to find Speaking Rain. She had so much to tell her sister.

Kaya found Speaking Rain in the snug winter lodge, twining cord from shredded hemp. Kaya went to her knees in front of her and placed her hands on Speaking Rain's arm. "Tawts may-we, Little Sister," Kaya breathed. "I'm here again!"

"Tawts may-we!" Speaking Rain gently touched Kaya's fingers. "Is that pine pitch I smell on your hands? Did you get hurt?"

"My hands and arms got burned by falling embers, but I treated the burns with medicine that my name-sake taught me to make," Kaya said. "You were right to be troubled about fires!"

Speaking Rain drew in a sharp breath. "What happened?"

Sitting close to her sister's side, Kaya told how she'd found Steps High in the rogue stallion's herd, and about their escape from the fire. "When we got back to the hunting camp, everyone thought we were ghosts—covered in black from the smoke. Before we left that country, Toe-ta and some other men rounded up the other Nimíipuu horses," Kaya finished.

"And now you're back safely!" Speaking Rain had been listening intently, as though she could feel, and hear, and even see everything Kaya described. "Whistles! Your horse came to you because she recognized your whistle. Then the Stick People saved your lives with a whistle."

"Aa-heh," Kaya agreed. "We left the Stick People a big gift of kinnikinnick berries."

Speaking Rain clasped Kaya's shoulder. "Tell me about Brown Deer and Cut Cheek. Did he hunt well?"

"Cut Cheek's a strong hunter!" Kaya said excitedly. "Our parents agree that he and Brown Deer should marry. Eetsa's going to visit Cut Cheek's mother soon to plan the wedding trade. We'll have the marriage feast and gift exchange before the snow gets deep. But come with me now! Don't you want to stroke Steps High again? I know you love her, too. And you have to meet her foal! They're the most wonderful horses ever!"

When the time came for the wedding ceremony, the frozen ground was covered with lightly fallen snow. Brown Deer and the other women put up a lodge for the celebration, then began cooking for the wedding feast. Soon the air smelled deliciously of roasting meats, kouse and camas cakes, and berry dishes. Kaya's mouth watered as she helped carry the gifts her family had made to the new lodge.

"Here's the last of the bundles, Granddaughter," Kautsa said. She placed a large bag filled with dried roots into Kaya's outstretched arms, put another under her own arm, and picked up a torch. As she walked ahead, she left shallow footprints in the dusting of snow.

Kaya's skin prickled with anticipation as she followed her grandmother inside the empty lodge. Now it was cold and silent here, but when everyone gathered today it would be filled with happy talk and laughter. They'd feast until they couldn't eat any more. Then Brown Deer's family would give woven bags filled with dried berries, roots, and camas to the groom's family—food the women had gathered and prepared. Matching them gift for gift, Cut Cheek's family would give parfleches filled with dried meat to the bride's people—foods contributed by the men.

Kautsa stacked the woven bags on top of the large

pile of gifts already resting on the tule mats. "There, that's everything," she said with satisfaction. "Now we're ready! Let me light one of these fires to warm up the place a little. I want to stay here for a while, don't you? We've been so busy lately that we haven't had time to talk."

As Kautsa knelt to light the fire, Kaya gazed at her grandmother's kind face. Her black hair was streaked with gray and her forehead and cheeks were deeply creased. Firelight glittered in her dark eyes. "Have I ever told you about the time I got lost on the mountainside—truly, completely lost?" she asked Kaya.

Kaya smiled. She loved her grandmother's stories. "When was that, Kautsa?"

"As you might imagine, it was when I was a little girl, about the age of the twins." Kautsa sat back on her heels as the fire began to crackle and held out her hands to the warmth. "I was walking back from picking berries with my mother when she discovered her workbag was missing. She was upset and wanted to go back to look for it. But she didn't want to carry the heavy berry baskets, so she put them down on the trail and told me to sit by them. She made me promise to wait patiently for her and not to move, not even a little bit. She said she wouldn't be long, and she started back up the trail.

"I sat there for what seemed like a long time. I was hot and thirsty and bored. Mosquitoes bit me, and deerflies buzzed around my head. After a while I got up and began poking around in the bushes, looking for something to do. I walked a little way into the under-brush, then a little farther, and a little farther yet. All of a sudden, I realized I didn't know where I was. I tried to get back to the trail, but I couldn't find it. I was lost! Then I forgot everything I'd been told to do if I got lost. Instead of staying right where I was and waiting to be found, I started to run.

"I ran downhill, thorns tearing at my dress, twigs scratching my arms and my face. There were no trails there, no sign that anyone had passed that way. I thought I would never see my family again, so I started to cry, 'Toe-ta! Eetsa! Help me, help me!' I called to them until I couldn't run any farther. Then I curled up under a bush and sobbed until I fell asleep.

"That's where I was, asleep, when my older brother found me. He was hunting higher on the mountain when he heard my cries. He knew that sound travels upward, so he rode down, following my sobs. He took me to our camp. I was overjoyed to see my mother again! She put willow bark on all my cuts and insect bites. She washed my face and fed me. Then she called Whipwoman to teach me my lesson!" Kautsa laughed, and Kaya laughed with her.

Then Kautsa put her hand on Kaya's. "I told you that story for a reason. What lesson do you think my mother wanted me to learn?"

"Not to disobey her," Kaya answered confidently.

"Aa-heh, that's one lesson," Kautsa went on, "but there was another one. She wanted me to learn to be patient—to wait, and to trust the wisdom of others. That's a very difficult thing to do, for it takes great strength to wait patiently." She thought for a moment, then went on. "Granddaughter, you've already faced many tests of bravery. Your next test will be one of patience, and of trusting the wisdom of our elders."

Kaya frowned. "What do you mean, Kautsa?"

"I'm speaking of your vision quest, Granddaughter —the vigil you must keep at the sacred place on the mountain," Kautsa said. "If your spirit is clear and you're prepared—and if you can hold on and not run away—then your wyakin will come to you there. But before that happens you'll be hungry and thirsty, and exhausted from fasting and praying day and night. Are you afraid?"

Kaya clasped her elbows, asking herself, *Am I afraid?* She had certainly been afraid when enemies captured her. She had been afraid when she escaped and found her way home. She'd been frightened to think she'd lost her sister, and her horse. And she'd been terrified when she was chased by the forest fire. But what she felt now wasn't fear—it was determination. "I'm not afraid, Kautsa," she said in a firm voice. "I'm ready to meet whatever comes."

"Why, that's exactly what your namesake would have said!" Kautsa exclaimed. "You're more like her than you may know. Soon, I believe, you'll use her name. It will be so good for her name to come alive again!"

Kaya's chest felt warm with gratitude when she thought again of Swan Circling's gift. Kaya wanted so much to take the name of her hero, and now her grandmother felt that the time was almost here.

From across the village, criers began calling out, "Visitors are coming! Get ready to greet them!"

"Saddle up your horse and go meet Cut Cheek's people," Kautsa said, getting to her feet. "I'll light these other fires and make the lodge warm for our feast. Go on now, be quick! We've talked enough."

Kaya ran to get the beautiful saddle she'd received at the giveaway after Swan Circling's burial. Then she hurried to the horse herd nearby. Tatlo bounded along with her, snapping at snowflakes and tossing up fallen snow with his nose. Steps High was pawing through the ice for grass with the other horses. When she heard Kaya's whistle, she trotted to her side, snorting white plumes of breath.

Kaya thought her horse seemed almost as excited as her frisky dog. Kaya pressed her cheek to Steps High's muzzle and stroked her horse's chest, feeling the strong, loyal heart beating there. In response, Steps High arched her neck and nudged Kaya's shoulder. As Kaya cinched the saddle tightly, Sparks Flying crowded against his mother, head high and ears forward as though he were eager to welcome visitors, too.

Kaya swung up into the saddle and settled her

feet in the stirrups. "Come on, girl," she said to her horse, and then slapped her leg to signal Tatlo to stay at her side. Urging Steps High into a run, Kaya galloped out to meet the visitors on their horses appearing over the horizon.

INSIDE Kaya's World

In the same way Kaya knew to be careful when she smelled smoke on the wind, many Nez Perce people had visions that warned them to be careful of the people with pale faces who were beginning to come to their homeland.

Most Nez Perces saw their first white people in the fall of 1805, when Kaya would have been 50 years old. That's when the men of the Lewis and Clark Expedition stumbled out of the Bitterroot Mountains and into a Nez Perce camp. The explorers were starving and freezing. The Nez Perce befriended the travelers and helped them resume their journey. In later years, white missionaries and settlers came to Nez Perce country and were treated kindly, too.

In the 1840s, white *prospectors*, or people searching for gold, began trickling through Nez Perce country on the Oregon Trail. Some were infected with smallpox, measles, or other diseases that killed thousands of Nez Perces. That trickle of white people became a flood in 1850, when gold was discovered in the Northwest.

Over the next 30 years, the United States government took away most of the Nez Perces' homeland so that white people could settle on it. The settlers cut down forests and let their pigs eat the camas Nez Perces depended on for food. The government set aside a small tract of land in Idaho for all Nez Perce people to live on called the Nez Perce Reservation.

The U.S. government tried to force Indians on reservations to *assimilate*—to give up their traditional ways and live like white people. Children were put into missionary schools to learn English and were punished if they spoke their own language. The reservation land was divided into small parcels and given to individual Indians to make a living by farming instead of hunting and gathering for their food.

The Nez Perce have lost much over the last 200 years, but they have never lost their spirit. History has scattered the people to different reservations and all over the world, breaking bonds that had been built over generations. Yet, as the Nez Perce saying goes, "Wherever we go, we are always Nez Perce."

The Nez Perce people have worked hard to keep their culture alive and strong. Today, Nez Perce children continue to hear the legends and learn the songs, dances, and arts of their people. They proudly carry on the traditions of their ancestors, and one day they will pass them on to their own children.

If Kaya lived among the Nez Perce people today, she'd be happy to see that many of them still live on the same land she called home. She'd be glad to hear her language being spoken, smell salmon roasting on the fire, and step inside a longhouse to hear legends and stories. She'd be especially proud to watch the young girls, so much like herself, parade their beautiful horses in honor of their ancestors, whose inspiring spirits live on to strengthen and nourish all Nez Perce people.

GLOSSARY of Nez Perce Words

In the story, Nez Perce words are spelled so that English readers can pronounce them. Here, you can also see how the words are actually spelled and said by the Nez Perce people.

PHONETIC/ NEZ PERCE	PRONUNCIATION	MEANING
aa-heh/´éehe	*AA-heh*	yes, that's right
Eetsa/Iice	*EET-sah*	mother
Hun-ya-wat/ Hanyaw´áat	*hun-yah-WAHT*	the Creator
katsee-yow-yow/ qe´ci´yew´yew´	*KAHT-see-yow-yow*	thank you
Kautsa/Qáaca´c	*KOUT-sah*	grandmother from mother's side
Kaya´aton´my´	*ky-YAAH-a-ton-my*	she who arranges rocks
Nimíipuu	*nee-MEE-poo*	The People; known today as the Nez Perce
Pi-lah-ka/Piláqá	*pee-LAH-kah*	grandfather from mother's side
Salish/Sélix	*SAY-leesh*	friends of the Nez Perce who live near them
Tatlo	*TAHT-lo*	ground squirrel
tawts/ta´c	*TAWTS*	good

tawts may-we/ ta´c méeywi	*TAWTS MAY-wee*	good morning
tee-kas/tikée´s	*tee-KAHS*	baby board, or cradleboard
Toe-ta/Toot´a	*TOH-tah*	father
Wallowa/ Wal´áwa	*wah-LAU-wa*	Wallowa Valley in present-day Oregon
wapalwaapal	*WAH-pul-WAAH-pul*	western yarrow, a plant that helps stop bleeding
wyakin/ wéeyekin	*WHY-ah-kin*	guardian spirit

Read more of KAYA'S stories,
available from booksellers and at *americangirl.com*

❈ *Classics* ❈
Kaya's classic series, now in two volumes:

Volume 1:
The Journey Begins
When Kaya and her blind
sister are captured by enemy
raiders, it takes all of her
courage and skill to survive.
If she escapes, will she ever see
her sister—and her Appaloosa
mare, Steps High—again?

Volume 2:
Smoke on the Wind
Kaya's pup, Tatlo, gives her
comfort while she searches for
her lost sister and her beloved
horse, Steps High. When a
forest fire threatens all she
holds dear, Kaya must face her
greatest fear yet.

❈ *Journey in Time* ❈
Travel back in time—and spend a day with Kaya!

The Roar of the Falls
What's it like to live in Kaya's world? Ride bareback, sleep in
a tepee, and help Kaya train a filly—but watch out for bears!
Choose your own path through this multiple-ending story.

❈ *Mystery* ❈
Another thrilling adventure with Kaya!

The Silent Stranger
During the winter Spirit Dances, a strange woman appears in
Kaya's village. Why is she alone, and why will she not speak?
To find out the truth, Kaya must look deep into her own heart.

※ A Sneak Peek at ※

The Roar of
the Falls

My Journey with Kaya

Meet Kaya and take an unforgettable journey
in a book that lets *you* decide what happens.

open my eyes. Bright sunlight makes me blink. My bedroom is gone, and I'm sprawled on a patch of damp grass somewhere outside. I push myself up out of the mud and stand up slowly, dizzy from all the spinning. I can't quite believe what I see. A broad river rushes by, feeding a giant waterfall, bigger than any I've ever seen. The water crashes over black rocks and fills my ears with its roar. On both sides of the water, the grassy riverbanks are covered with hundreds of shelters. Some look like tepees, and others are huts in different shapes and sizes. They stretch as far down the river as I can see. Steep bluffs rise behind me. Footpaths meander up the sides of the bluffs, and at the top, I can see horses grazing on the flatlands.

I'm no longer wearing striped pajamas. Instead, I have on some kind of brown leather dress that's decorated with delicate white shells. Fringe hangs from the front and along the hem. Lace-up leather moccasins wrap around my feet and calves. I recognize only one thing: the shell bracelet on my wrist.

My heart is pounding in my chest. Where am I? What just happened? *Don't panic*, I tell myself. I close my eyes and take five long, slow breaths. When I open my eyes, I'm still next to the roaring river, but I feel a bit calmer. Wherever I am, I can't just stand here in the mud. My damp moccasins slide as I make my way carefully along the riverbank. There's a steep drop to the water below, and I'm still a little dizzy.

I see people in the distance. Their clothes are like mine, and everyone has deep brown skin and dark hair, which they wear in two braids—even the boys. I realize that the people look like the pictures of American Indians I've seen in my school textbooks. *How is this possible?* I wonder as a group of children run past with what look like toy bows and arrows. Am I—could I—be in another time?

The overpowering roar of the waterfall makes my head ache. I'm confused and my legs are weak. I stumble, going down to my knees. I've strayed too close to the steep edge. Suddenly, the ground gives way beneath me and I'm slipping down the riverbank. Desperately, I cry out, clutching loose rocks and soil, sliding toward the crashing water below.

Someone catches my arm. "Hold my hand!" a voice cries. I look up to see a girl's face above me. She clutches my wrist and pulls, and I claw my way back up the bank. Panting, I collapse on the soft grass.

"Thank you," I gasp, pushing myself up to my knees. The girl takes my arm and helps me to my feet.

I stare at the girl in wonder. She looks about my age, with black braids that reach almost to her waist and dark almond-shaped eyes that twinkle. She wears a leather dress, too, with fringes like mine, and the same moccasins.

She's staring back at me with concern. "Your face and arms are scraped," she says. "You're covered in mud, too," she says. "I'll help you get cleaned up. Where is your family's camp?"

"Camp?" I say tentatively.

The girl sweeps her arm over the clusters of shelters spread along the riverbank. "Your camp is with the rest of the *Nimíipuu*, isn't it?"

"*Nimíipuu?*" I ask. It seems like I should know what that means, but I don't.

"Of course you're *Nimíipuu*—we speak the same language." She looks at me curiously. "But we've never met," she continues.

"I—I don't really know what's happened," I stammer. It's impossible to think over the roar of the falls and the strange twist of events. I don't want to lie, but I don't think I should tell this girl that I was transported here from my bedroom. "I just—found myself here," I say truthfully.

The girl takes my arm. "You have been frightened by your fall. You are confused. Come to my camp with me. It's not far from here. My grandmother will know what to do." The girl's brow is knit with concern. "I'm Kaya," she adds.

"Kaya," I repeat, my voice filled with gratitude. "You saved my life!" I look down the crumbled section of riverbank to the crashing, foaming water below. My stomach flops over with a nauseating twist. "That was so courageous. You could have fallen, too!"

Kaya cocks her head to one side. "*Nimíipuu* always look out for each other. That's what my grandmother says." She takes my hand and squeezes it. I can feel how strong she is.

I try not to look shocked. This girl just risked her own life to help a total stranger and now she's acting like it's not that big a deal. Does this happen all the time around here? Do people just swoop in and pluck one another from danger?

The reality of my strange situation crashes over me once more. Where is my family? Where is my home? Where am I? I sink down onto a nearby rock, trying to sort out my swimming thoughts.

"Are you unwell?" Kaya asks. "Perhaps you hit your head when you slipped. I could get Bear Blanket—she's a healer." She turns as if to run.

"No, wait." I reach out and catch Kaya's hand before she dashes off. "It's not my head. I—I—" What I really need is a chance to think for a moment alone. "Maybe just a drink of water."

Kaya pats my shoulder. "I will get water. Rest here." She dashes down the path toward the shelters.

As she disappears, I slide off the rock and onto the ground on the other side so that I'm shielded from the path. I need to be alone. I need to think. First I was in my bedroom. I was sitting on the bed. I had made this bracelet. I look down at my wrist. Right before this thing happened, I had just put it on. Then I was touching the shell, just like this. I trace a circle around the rim of the shell with one finger and suddenly, I'm spun dizzily, whirling again, the world in blackness.

I land with a thump onto something soft and fuzzy and open my eyes. I'm lying on the carpet in my bedroom, wearing my pajamas. My jewelry-making things are spread out by my bed, right where I left them. The roar of the falls is gone. Instead, I can hear my father practicing scales down in the living room. The phone is ringing in my mom's study. Everything is just as it was when I left. It seems to be the same moment I left.

Have I been in another world? I know I was wearing a leather dress. I met a girl named Kaya. But now I'm back in my own room, and no time has passed. I'm wearing my own clothes again, and there are no signs of scrapes on my arms or face.

I look down at the bracelet on my wrist. Whatever is happening, the bracelet's doing it. Well, I'm doing it. I sent myself to that other world when I rubbed the shell, and that's how I got home. I could do it again!

Kaya's flashing eyes and friendly smile swim up in front of me. I'm surprised to realize that I want to leave the comfortable familiarity of my room and get to know the girl who saved my life.

Excitement seizes me as I place my fingertip on the shell. Holding my breath, I trace a circle around its edge. Once again, the room spins around me. I close my eyes, and when I open them, I'm on the grass, sitting behind the big rock, wearing the same muddy dress and damp moccasins. I'm back! But I can get home—as long as I have this bracelet.

About the Author

When JANET SHAW was a girl, she
and her brother liked to act out stories,
especially ones about sword fights and wild
horses. Today, Ms. Shaw lives in North
Carolina with her husband. Their two dogs
sleep at her feet when she's writing.

About the Advisory Board

American Girl extends its deepest appreciation
to the advisory board that authenticated Kaya's stories.